WHEN THE CEILING IS ZERO

by

Robert D. Foster

MOODY PRESS
CHICAGO

© 1973 by
THE MOODY BIBLE INSTITUTE
OF CHICAGO

ISBN: 0-8024-9433-1

The use of selected references from various versions of the Bible in this publication does not necessarily imply publisher endorsement of the versions in their entirety.

Printed in the United States of America

CONTENTS

PART		PAGE
1.	A Challenge from Job	5
2.	A Challenge from Psalms	35
3.	A Challenge from Proverbs	67
4.	A Challenge from Ecclesiastes	99
5.	A Challenge from Isaiah	129

Part 1

A CHALLENGE FROM JOB

When the ceiling is zero

Here is an opportunity to look into the classroom where God is training and building men. See how He works, observe His methods, listen to His instruction.

Job is a man learning the lessons of his own nothingness in the fierce fire of deep affliction through loss, bereavement, and disease; fighting single-handed against the crude philosophy and cruel attacks of his friends; above all, with his own proud, unsubdued self-righteousness and unbelief. At last, God breaks through and leads Job to the point where he listens and learns the lesson of all the ages, that He alone is God. Therein lies Job's blessing.

You will find no easy answers, but when problems close in and the ceiling is zero, you will learn as Job did that the Lord is the one to turn to in order that your life may fulfill the purpose which He lovingly planned for you.

SHAKEN, BUT NOT REMOVED

"There was a man in the land of Uz, whose name was Job."
Job 1:1

God is in the business of shaking men. The effect is shocking for there is little in most of us that remains unshakable. Quivering and shivering we so easily come unglued at the seams of life. Needed: men who cannot be shaken loose from their moorings!

Such was the man from Uz, Job, wealthy, happy, honorable and upright. This stately, sturdy and spiritual tree-of-a-man was loaded with fruit. Profuse were the blossoms and branches of his life—ever bearing, ever prospering.

One day he was stripped of all! Satan, the sly one, said to God, "Your friend Job is a religious fraud. It pays him to be religious. Rob him of his wealth and health and he will renounce You."

Job became a test case to demonstrate the strength of faith. Can that which we believe be affected by that which we possess? Is our success the cause of our confidence in the Almighty?

God hedges about those whom He loves. The enemy subtly suggests, "Remove that bulkhead and watch him fall. Allow me and my vanguards to strip him and we will finish him off. He will curse the very God he now worships."

Divine permission was granted. The hedge was removed and Chaldeans, Sabeans, fire, wind, and sickness increased Job's troubles to monstrous proportions.

The real man is revealed as surface things are removed. With his coat torn away, his spiritual muscles were flexed. With disease in his body, Job continued to praise God. When all would seem lost, the unshakable remained!

Shaken but not removed. Chapter 19 and verse 28 has the answer: "The root of the matter is found in me." Blossoms and branches were gone but the root system remained.

God allowed the fire to reveal the pure gold in Job. The howling winds of circumstantial temptations will soon reveal if a man is a "cut flower" character—beautiful to look upon but without roots.

"Who can separate us from the love of Christ? Can trouble, pain or persecution? Can lack of clothes and food, danger to life and limb, the threat of force of arms? No, in all these things we win an overwhelming victory through him who has proved His love for us" (Ro 8:35, 37, Phillips).

WHY, LORD, WHY?

"The Lord gave, and the Lord hath taken away; blessed be the name of the Lord. In all this Job sinned not, nor charged God foolishly." JOB 1:21-22

Daily dilemmas that cause a man's heart to thump and tie his stomach up in knots completely bewilder and bog us down with the question, "Why, Lord, why?"

One hundred years ago, when British missionaries were first going to India, their leader, Dr. James Cope, died on the high seas. Not knowing the language, people or culture of the new country, the advice of Calcutta businessmen was, "Take the first ship back to England."

One of the young recruits for Christ replied, "That's out of the question. I came here to preach the gospel, and, God helping me, I mean to do it."

To this came the response, "If you bring God into the decision, that alters it altogether." (As if you could leave God out!)

No night is too dark for God, no knot too complicated for Him to untie. He is the perfect problem solver. God knows all the details behind every "Why?"

Job lost all but his life, only to gain back from the hand of God twice as much. This powerful prince of the desert knew what it meant to be in difficulty but never forgot who had allowed it all to happen!

Paul, the apostle, must have remembered the Job story when he, too, had lost all things. See Philippians 3:8. You are never the loser when your life's predicaments are committed to God.

In 2 Chronicles 25 is the story of King Amaziah. When God asked this man to lose some two hundred thousand dollars that he had paid out to a neighboring nation, He assured him that He was able to return much more than to him than he had lost.

Like Job, our needs are many. We continually ask, "Why?"

Bring God into the center of every matter. If He finds that you are solid gold and not just electroplated, then you can claim the promise, "We know also that those who love God, those who have been called in terms of His purpose, have His aid and interest in everything" (Ro 8:28, Moffatt).

ROLL IT AND LEAVE IT

"For what I fear comes upon me, and what I dread befalls me. I am not at ease, nor am I quiet, and I am not at rest, but turmoil comes." JOB 3:25-26 (NASB)

Do you find yourself under the weight and burden of daily problems? Are you seeking an escape from this day's circumstances?

Bring God into the picture! "Roll your work onto the Lord and your plans will be achieved" (Pr 16:3, Berkeley).

This is a promise from the Promiser. You do your part of rolling, and He will do His part—achieving. If you want success, there must be substitution. You just are not big enough to do the job.

Roll not only your burdens, your problems, your overwhelming difficulties onto the Lord, but give to Him the big and little, the projects you can handle and the ones you cannot.

Hand over with hands off! "Commit your way to the LORD, trust also in Him, and He will do it" (Ps 37:5, NASB).

Here is a really practical suggestion. After rolling your work onto the Lord, be sure to leave it there. Commit it safely into His keeping. Take Him into partnership and the work which was once a burden and weight, is upon His shoulders. "You can throw the whole weight of your anxieties upon him, for you are his personal concern" (1 Pe 5:7, Phillips).

You will never roll from your heart and shoulders what you are carrying unless you recognize onto whom you can roll this day's entire work. He is the Lord, the Creator of heaven and earth. The one who formed the mountains and the valleys with His fingers. He scooped out the oceans with His hands.

His name is El Shaddai—"The Almighty One."

His name is Jehovah-jireh—"The Lord will provide."

TAKE HEART, FAINTHEART

Job's reply: "Oh, that my sadness and troubles were weighed. For they are heavier than the sand of a thousand seashores. . . . For I am utterly helpless, without any hope." JOB 6:1-3, 13 (Living Bible)

How often have you seen a man failing in his strength? The man of courage falls into the bog of discouragement; the strong becomes weak; the heavyweight shrivels down to nothingness; the Job goes from the heights to the depths.

A man like that is ripe for a good case of despondency and morbid depression. Satan knows the depths of the human heart. He will find mud there!

As with Job, two effects take place when things go sour:

You feel like a man thrown to the ground. Job sat deflated and depressed on his pile of ashes.

Secondly, you sense a disquieting spirit within your soul, a noisy restlessness that displays itself in grumbling, murmuring, and fits of complaining. "Why has this happened to me?"

Loneliness, financial problems, business pressures, and poor health can make you a candidate for a cast down and disquieted spirit!

Take heart, faintheart. Often those men who have climbed to tremendous heights, take a nose dive into the slough of despondency. The bigger they are, the harder they fall, but it does not always have to be so. What Job needed is your answer and mine from the heart and pen of the psalmist: "Hope thou in God: for I shall yet praise him for the help of his countenance" (Ps 42:5).

Do not magnify your problem or sorrow as the Israelites did after the spies investigated the Promised Land. "They are giants and we are but grasshoppers" (Num 13:33).

Not so Caleb and Joshua. They saw the problems and impossibilities but they also saw God. This gives perspective. God was between them and their problems.

"After you have suffered a little while, our God, who is full of kindness through Christ, will give you his eternal glory. He personally will come and pick you up, and set you firmly in place, and make you stronger than ever" (1 Pe 5:10, Living Bible).

SUFFICIENT GRACE

"My days are swifter than a weaver's shuttle, and they come to a hopeless end." JOB 7:6 (Berkeley)

Many a man's life is hopelessly mired in moral bankruptcy. Man's only hope for solvency is the grace of God. Grace is God's all for man's bankruptcy. Job's friends argued that God bestows favor on the righteous and afflicts the guilty. In order to be blessed, Job needed good deeds. But Job came to understand that God's grace is a free gift.

This grace of God saw his life like a weaver's shuttle coming to a hopeless end. When it seemed that every door had slammed shut in his face, grace bought the mortgage on his life and paid the bills completely.

All is of grace. It is all God's doing. Man need not attempt to do anything for his redemption because Christ has done everything.

Free grace is a sovereign gift provided for every contingency. It is unmerited and unending.

Job did not need justice but mercy. God met him when he had nothing and deserved nothing. And God promises him everything. "Grace is love stooping. Grace is divine energy in quest of unlovely men."

The Lord assures us as He did Job, "My grace is sufficient for thee. My strength is made perfect in weakness" (2 Co 12:9).

We come to the point in life when we discover that money is not sufficient. Neither is our learning, our culture, nor a penetrating personality. When life seems but a breath, God's grace alone is sufficient!

BRIDGING THE GAP

"There is no umpire between us, no middle man, no mediator to bring us together." JOB 9:33 (Living Bible)

Between man and God there exists a great gulf. What is the linkage between these two worlds of living? How can man reach the Holy God over on the far side?

This chasm has created a craving for bridge building. For thousands of years, religions have attempted to remove the canyon. Man has built tremendous cathedrals, offered gifts and sacrifices, and formulated creeds and rituals, yet in spite of all this, the gap has not been bridged! The human heart remains unsatisfied and restless.

God remains holy and righteous. The great gulf remains. Our life is human and carnal. His is supernatural and spiritual.

What can be done to bridge this gulf? Is a new dimension possible where man could live with God and receive His nature and see life in His perspective? Is there no umpire, no middle man, no mediator between God and man?

Jesus Christ, God's only begotten Son, steps into the gap. He became the bridge. The work of Christ on the cross of Calvary was man's reconciliation to God. Grace has bridged the gulf. Whereas sin had separated, the sacrifice of His blood is man's only chance for reconciliation.

This is the bridge that love built! This is the bridge of conversion, redemption and mediation. No longer must man try to get to God in his way. God has come to man in His way: "I am the Way."

In need of an umpire, middle man, mediator? Are you in need of a Saviour from your sin to unite you to God?

Come to Jesus! Communication and communion are immediate. The gap is removed instantaneously. He is the only bridge by which mankind answers God's plea: Be reconciled!

"All this is God's doing, for He has reconciled us to himself through Jesus Christ; and he has made us agents of the reconciliation. . . . As his personal representatives we say, 'Make your peace with God' " (2 Co 5: 18, 20, Phillips).

NOT DIFFICULT BUT IMPOSSIBLE

"I am weary of living. Let me complain freely. I will speak in my sorrow and bitterness. I will say to God, 'Don't just condemn me . . . tell me why you are doing it.'"
JOB 10:1-2 (Living Bible)

"Don't tell me that worry doesn't do any good. I know better. The things I worry about don't happen."

Do not cross your bridges till you come to them.

Do not carry your burden till it is placed on your back.

Do not count your troubles till they are sent your way.

Dr. Charles Mayo tells us that worry and anxiety not only affect the heartbeat and blood circulation, but make man a candidate for the 219 diseases and 642 complications known to medicine. He never knew a man to die from overwork, but thousands die from worry and anxiety.

A worrier is a pessimist! He sees calamity in every business opportunity; he pays heavy interest on trouble before it comes due; he is impatient about circumstances and economic conditions that are beyond his power to control.

Job was worried about things that had happened and had not happened yet. His mental life was entwined with the suppositions of a difficult life.

Job never stopped to learn the root meaning of worry, "division." The worried heart is a divided heart. Job partly trusted God and partly looked at his circumstances. His future was dark and bleak. The pressures were heavy. A gnawing anxiety was his lot.

"Why worry? There is a simplicity about God in working out His plans, yet a resourcefulness equal to any difficulty, and an unswerving faithfulness to His trusting child, and an unforgetting steadiness in holding to His purpose. It is safe to trust God's methods and go by His clock.

"Difficulty is the very atmosphere of miracle. . . . It is miracle in its first stage. If it is to be a great miracle, the condition is not difficulty but impossiblity!" (S. D. Gordon).

To this God of the impossible take all your worries and cares. If we do not pray about everything, we will usually worry about everything. If something is big enough to cause upset and fretfulness, it is big enough to talk to God about.

The alternative to worry is worship. Weary of living? Have faith in the living God!

"Throw all your anxiety onto Him, for His concern is about you" (1 Pe 5:7, Berkeley).

SHAKEN, BUT NOT SHOOK

"Behold, God tears down, and it cannot be built again; He shuts a man in, and none can open." JOB 12:14 (Berkeley)

Have you ever noticed the instructions on the back of a bottle of salad dressing? "Shake well before using!"

Hand lotion, shoe polish, and floor cleaner—these and a host of other everyday items need agitation to be at their best. Without the shaking, you have nothing but a thin oil or paste.

Life is no different. There must be some shaking on the eve of usefulness. It could almost be an axiom for your life: service is in direct relation to shaking.

But we do not want to be shaken. These are days for settling back and being at ease. Cozy and Snug are twin brothers in the successful and prosperous life image. Storms, stirrings and strife upset the well-oiled routine that most of us are seeking.

Is this a principle of the Creator with His children: usefulness relies upon the shakings of life?

Job was a shaken man. Jonah was shaken too. The bottom dropped out of his self-laid plans and it was a long way down before he hit bottom and bounced back up.

Peter was shaken from the peaceful fishing on the Sea of Galilee to the stimulating events of the book of Acts.

Moab needed stirring. It had gone stale through inactivity, lethargy and haughty independence. "Moab has been at ease from his youth and has settled on his lees; he has not been emptied from vessel to vessel, nor has he gone into exile; so his taste remains in him, and his scent is not changed" (Jer 48:11). The sediment at the bottom of a wine vat accumulates and remains in its place when it is not cleaned out. What a smell! What a slothful waste!

Yes, the almighty God is in the business of shaking men and nations for their good and His glory.

"He will sift out everything without solid foundation, so that only unshakable things will be left. . . . Let us please God by serving Him with thankful hearts, and with holy fear and awe" (Heb 12:27-28, Living Bible).

THE ART OF BEING A SPONGE

"Oh, please be quiet! That would be your highest wisdom."
                                    JOB 13:5 (Living Bible)

Have you found it a struggle to listen? Is sixty seconds a suffocatingly long time to keep quiet?

The editors of *Fortune* Magazine polled the wives of some business executives and discovered that listening to their husbands was their number one duty.

Listening is a ministry.

C. G. Trumbull has a thrilling chapter on how to win a hearing in his little book *Taking Men Alive*. He says that more men can be won over by listening and showing genuine interest in another than with a talkative attitude that says "I'm going to help you."

Listening is active. Most men must be classified as half-listeners. The three friends of Job listened just long enough to be polite and then started on their remedy. They only half-listened to Job while they thought of their replies.

In Job 16:1-4 the one needing help cries: "I have heard all this before. What miserable comforters all of you are." (Living Bible)

Unburdening is important. Often you may be asked to offer advice or give solutions to a problem. Your friend may not want your advice or counsel at all. He might just want the opportunity to talk freely. He needs to listen to his own thoughts as they are put into words.

This is the ministry in listening quietly and objectively—the highest wisdom! The art of being a sounding board, not a cross examiner, but a sponge.

Don't sit in judgment, ready to pounce. If you would be a good listener, be outwardly shock-proof.

Men so often think they must always contribute something when they are in the company of others, that this is the one service they have to render. They forget that listening can be a greater service than speaking.

Develop the art of keeping a gracious and loving open ear.

"Let every man be swift to hear, slow to speak" (Ja 1:19).

THE BAROMETER OF BENDABLENESS

"I was living quietly until he broke me apart. He has taken me by the neck and dashed me to pieces, then hung me up as his target." JOB 16:12 (Living Bible)

Learn to live a flexible life. Our need is to be identified but cautious about being identical. No one wants to live in a rut, but we must avoid the danger of rebelling against the status quo just for the sake of change.

This is a challenge for adaptability, flexibility. We must take care to avoid rigidity that would keep us from adapting to a variety of strange and difficult circumstances.

"I have learned to be content, whatever the circumstances may be" (Phil 4:11, Phillips). That is the apostle Paul preaching. He could go from pulpit to prison and not miss a stroke. On top or on the bottom, in poverty or in plenty, abased or abounding, in misunderstanding, criticism, and disappointment, Paul knew the value of flexibility.

The size of a man is determined by the size of the thing it takes to get him down.

Adaptability is a great challenge to your personal pride. Job gave testimony, "I was living quietly until. . ." God entered the arena of his life and challenged Job's ideas and plans for the future. The invigorating antidote for stagnation is the gracious plan of Almighty God for your life. This is the barometer of bendableness. It may not be in your plans but the Lord will place you in the classroom where you learn to live flexibly.

David could move from the palace to his father's sheepfold because of flexibility of spirit. Phillip left a citywide evangelistic crusade for the solitary witness in the desert. The ability to fit in comes from bending to the Spirit.

Men who have ventured into realms of victory have not been characterized by hearts of stone nor of putty, but the adaptability and malleability of plastic, soft enough to be molded, yet capable of sturdiness and permanency in all form or place. Are you learning the lessons of flexibility?

"I am ready for anything through the strength of the one who lives within me" (Phil 4:13, Phillips).

NOT SOMEHOW, BUT TRIUMPHANTLY

"The righteous shall move onward and forward; those with pure hearts shall become stronger and stronger."
JOB 17:9 (Living Bible)

Welcome trials and troubles as friends. Do not resist them as enemies to your cozy and snug way of life.

The reason for this uncommon philosophy is found in the Holy Scriptures: "We also exult in our tribulations; knowing that tribulation brings about perseverance" (Ro 5:3, NASB).

Another word for perseverance is fortitude—the end result of pressure.

The pressure of finances, difficult circumstances, sorrow and heartache, unpopularity and loneliness tend to press you out of shape. These pressures can produce a spirit that does not just passively endure, but actively overcomes and conquers.

Fortitude—the God-given ability to face the storms of life head-on and come out not somehow, but triumphantly. "I do not like crises," said Lord Reith, "but I do like the opportunities they provide."

Fortitude—out of the battle you emerge stronger, purer and nearer to the heart of God.

When Sir Walter Scott was involved in ruin because of the bankruptcy of his publishers, he said, "No man will say 'poor fellow' to me; my own right hand will pay the debt." That is fortitude.

Someone once said to a gallant soul who was undergoing a great sorrow: "Sorrow fairly colors life, doesn't it?" Back came the reply: "Yes, it does, but I propose to choose the color!" That is fortitude.

One of my most beloved friends was shot through the throat during World War II. Doctors told him he could never talk again. Today Bob is preaching, teaching and witnessing to Japanese people in their own homeland. This is Christian fortitude!

"I pray that out of the glorious richness of his resources he will enable you to know the strength of the Spirit's inner reinforcement" (Eph 3:16, Phillips).

KNOWLEDGE IS SAFETY

"But as for me, I know that my Redeemer lives, and that he will stand upon the earth at last." JOB 19:25 (Living Bible)

Throughout their Los Angeles freight yards, the Southern Pacific Railroad had this motto: "If you do not know, you are not safe!"

Safety is in direct proportion to knowledge. Fatal mistakes result from not only, "Oops, I goofed!" but more likely, "No one ever told me."

The lyrics are the same in railroading, water safety, fire control or the eternal destiny of your soul. It pays to be properly informed.

The odds are stacked against any man while he plays the guessing game. To know is safety, happiness and enjoyment.

Take a look at Job. Chapter 19 is the story of a man almost-thrown. "He hath fenced up my way. . . . He hath stripped me. . . . He hath destroyed me. . . . He hath put my brethren far from me. . . . The hand of God hath touched me." Yet, in these fluctuating circumstances Job could say, "I know that my Redeemer liveth."

Is that mere bullheaded presumption, a cocky cliché of some religionist? Not at all! It is the sureness and security of a man who has had every doubt removed. No longer does he stumble in his thinking. No longer does he guess. Many things were unknown to Job, but of one thing he was sure—his Redeemer was alive!

An old warrior of the sea was asked: "Where did you find God?" Without hesitation or doubt there came the clear-cut answer: "Latitude 25, Longitude 54." That old sailor was safe because he knew!

In the last generation we have learned new and amazing facts about our universe. We have conquered diseases and invented comforts and conveniences by the score. Yet there remains insecurity, mental misery and spiritual darkness.

Only with an intimate knowledge of Jesus Christ will your quest for knowledge be fully satisfied. "I know whom I have trusted and I am absolutely sure that He is able to guard what I have entrusted to Him until that day" (2 Ti 1:12, Williams).

THE REFINING POT OF TRIALS

"Note this: Men are not the architects of their own fortune."
JOB 21:16 (Berkeley)

God needed a man of courage, conviction, and character. Where could He find a man with such high qualifications?

God chose Job of the land of Uz to pass the test worked out in the courts of heaven.

Job adjusted himself to every external circumstance and developed an inner growth through transplanting.

The financial crisis in the collapse of his agricultural empire; the personal dilemma in the death of all his children; the physical calamity of puss-filled boils that covered his body; the social affliction of his three so-called "comforters" were the difficulties he suffered.

Job learned the hard way that there is no butterfly without the struggle in the cocoon; no summer without the storms of winter; no feast without a sacrifice. If Job had missed out on even one of his "tough breaks" he would have been the loser. Character was matured by trial, strengthened by discipline, and enriched by disappointments.

"He is happy whose circumstances suit his temper; but he is more excellent who can suit his temper to any circumstances" (Hume).

Circumstances do not make or break you, they simply reveal your true character. To relate all of life to God is the secret of successful living. God put His human hunk of clay, Job, into His refining pot of trial and temptation. There came forth a vessel of gold that could say to generations of men to follow, "Men, we don't call the shots of life. God is involved. He is the divine architect of my fortune and yours!"

God has sovereign sway over all events. Every situation is known to Him. Sickness, financial setback, family misunderstanding, life's dark hours—all these happen within a framework of His purposes. No matter what the predicament...God is still God!

"Do not throw away your confidence; it carries a rich reward" (Heb 10:35, Berkeley).

GOD MAKES NO CARBON COPIES

"His mind concerning me remains unchanged, and who can turn him from his purposes? Whatever he wants to do, he does. So he will do to me all he has planned, and there is more ahead." JOB 23:13, 14 (Living Bible)

Beetles to boa constrictors; sunflowers to snapdragons; polliwogs to pickerels amply prove that our God is the God of variety.

There is nothing drab or colorless about Him or His creation. From His color tones and harmony, to the boundlessness of sizes, shapes, varieties and smells, how can one say that life is humdrum?

It is man-made machinery that produces uniformity. Nature gives infinite variety. Living without the Lord produces a monotonous existence.

Did you hear about the man who got so disgusted about having to dress and undress himself day after day that he finally committed suicide to escape from the necessity? He was that bored with repetition.

God makes originals, no carbon copies. "Old things pass away, behold, all things become new" (2 Co 5:17). The reporting magazine for the show world is interestingly called *Variety,* seeking new acts and actors to break through the unvaried monotony.

Men without God live lives that are like flat, barren desert. Oh, for a hill or valley to break the straightness of the line.

The way to keep the common from becoming commonplace, the familiar from becoming tiresome is to tie all things in with Jesus Christ. If His creation of nature can be so infinitely varied, how much more could our lives be unique as individual parts of His creation in harmony with His will.

"For I have learned to be content in whatever circumstances I am. . . . I have learned the secret. . . . I can do all things through Him who strengthens me" (Phil 4:11-13, NASB).

THINGS DO NOT JUST HAPPEN

"Why doesn't God open the court and listen to my case? Why must the godly wait for Him in vain?" JOB 24:1 (Living Bible)

Do you ever seem to be up against a brick wall with no visible way through? All is black, bleak and uncertain! At that moment you take a single step in faith and the way is opened.

Providence is God's way of allowing us to stand upon the brink of a precipice and then in the nick of time, when another step would be fatal, He stretches out His strong right arm and saves.

This concern and care of our heavenly Father caused Benjamin Franklin to reflect, "The longer I live, the more convincing proofs I see of this truth—that God governs in the affairs of men; and if a sparrow cannot fall to the ground without His notice, is it probable that an empire can rise without His aid?" This is the providence of our God.

Be thankful that in His providence you do not get all that you ask for. Shortsightedness fails to see the end. We see just the beginning or the middle, a faulty fragment. He sees the beginning from the end.

You have come a long way on the road with your Lord when you realize that things do not just happen. Life is not a gamble. Circumstances and events in your daily life are as threads in the eternal tapestry. The Lord God is the weaver. His purposes move on like the irresistible ocean current.

God misses nothing. If His eye is upon the falling sparrow, how much more He knows the perils of your daily walk—the wrongs that you suffer, the heartaches and loneliness through which you often pass.

"O men, how little you trust Him! Do not be troubled, then, and cry, 'What are we to eat?' or 'what are we to drink?' or 'how are we to be clothed?' . . . for your heavenly Father knows quite well you need all that" (Mt 6:31-32, Moffatt).

TIE A KNOT AND HANG ON!

"He it is Who spreads out the northern skies over emptiness and hangs the earth upon . . . nothing. Yet these are but a small part of His doings, the outskirts of His ways or the mere fringes of His force, the faintest whisper of His voice!"
JOB 26:7, 14 (Amplified)

When you come to the end of your rope, tie a knot and hang on! Aeronautically they call this flying blind! Nothing within the skill or senses of the pilot can know where he is or what he should do. This is the spot where he hands over the control of the plane to someone or something that does know.

When the ceiling of circumstances is zero, what is your reaction?

Most men admit to the empty feeling in the pit of their stomach. Others label it frustration and come apart at the emotional seams. A small minority concede it to be a hopeless situation but for God!

Meet my friend Job. Four thousand years ago he lived on Desperation Corner, not knowing which way to turn. In distress the Lord God is brought into view. He "hangeth the earth upon nothing."

In looking to God for deliverance of any kind, we are prone to try to discover what material He has on hand to work with in coming to our relief. If we are praying for financial help, we are apt to look over the community to see if we can think of anyone whom the Lord might influence to give us some money.

It is so human to look for something in sight that will help the Lord out. In time of need, if we can only find a little something for God to begin on, we seem so much better satisfied.

He needs nothing to begin with. In the beginning God created the heavens and the earth out of nothing.

When He made the earth, what did He hang it on? Nothing! No sky hooks.

The God who has made the earth, the sun, moon and stars out of nothing and has kept them hanging in space for thousands of years on nothing, cannot this God supply all your needs?

Trust Him to supply your needs out of nothing! "Thus far you have asked nothing in My name. Ask and you will receive, so that your joy may be complete" (Jn 16:24, Berkeley).

A CHRISTIAN IN SMALL THINGS

"Till I die I will not sacrifice my integrity."
                                    JOB 27:5 (Berkeley)

The cadets of the U.S. Air Force Academy were told recently by one of the top generals: "The professional officer must be a man of many qualities, but possessing one basic quality mandatory of any officer in the military services, this is unqualified integrity."

"Integrity when once compromised is gone forever and is not replaceable. It is the true mark of a professional officer. A lack of basic integrity is completely unacceptable in the military services."

This leader was talking about honesty, truthfulness, uprightness, and a moral soundness. Job was talking about the same qualities.

Can you be too scrupulous? In this day of relativity and situational ethics you just cannot afford to make exceptions on divine requirements. Do not be flexible with your soul. Cheating, lying, skimping on your work, and "everybody-does-it" dishonesty are basic sins in a spineless and godless character.

Straight living realizes that the end does not justify the means. "Any way to get where you want to go" is a cancerous philosophy. To walk the line begins with the fiber of your inner character.

He who is a Christian in small things is not a small Christian.

"The integrity of the upright shall guide them" (Pr 11:3).

You cannot vulcanize integrity onto the tread of your soul. Honesty and right-living are recreated by the regeneration of the Holy Spirit.

Abe Lincoln was a tall, ugly country boy serving as a store clerk. Seemingly there was nothing on the outside to indicate that this lad would ever get out of the backwoods. One day an elderly lady was shortchanged. He had failed to give her enough and she had not noticed. Those few pennies belonged to her but she lived several miles from town. After closing the store for the day, he hiked out to the farm to return the money and apologize to the old lady.

Just a few pennies, but Abraham Lincoln moved onward and forward and daily became stronger and stronger. That same integrity showed up during the critical Civil War decisions.

"Happy are the utterly sincere, for they will see God!" (Mt 5:8, Phillips).

NOT TROUBLES BUT OPPORTUNITIES

"Oh, for the years gone by when God took care of me, when He lighted the way before me . . . when my projects prospered." JOB 29:2-3, 6-7 (Living Bible)

Of one thing you can be sure, there will always be heartaches and sorrow for any man who chooses to live close to God.

Most men I know have discovered that the road is rough, the opposition plays it tough and the path is thorny.

But take heart, my friend, these circumstances do not make a man, they simply reveal what is on the interior. Job proves that trouble is not always due to some particular sin; that theory of sickness and suffering is false.

Flood and furnace are sent your way so that character may be revealed and developed. As the adage states: "The ripest fruit grows against the roughest wall."

Have you caught yourself inwardly mumbling along with Job: "What happened to the good old days? God lighted my way; I walked safely through the darkness; the friendship of God was felt in my home; the Almighty was still with me; all my projects prospered. . . . I suppose there is some good purpose in all this sorrow but I surely have not figured it out!"

In grief, sorrow and loss, beware of questioning God. The greatest benefits in life are not things, but opportunities.

Testings are your sermons. Trials reveal your theology. Pain preaches to men you could never before reach.

May not God allow you to go down in order to lift others up as they see your unshaken faith in the changeless Christ?

What a privilege to look back on some difficult experience and know that God used it in not only your soul-growth but also in the lives of others who were observing from the side lines.

In his book, *Baffled To Fight Better,* Dr. Oswald Chambers writes: "I can well imagine the comfort from the book of Job as from another book; the comfort not of didactic solution, but of exact expression given to grief. All through the book of Job there is a heartbreaking devotion to God in the midst of inexplicable complexity of sorrow."

"But He said to me, 'My spiritual strength is sufficient, for it is only by means of conscious weakness that perfect power is developed' " (2 Co 12:9, Williams).

THE SECOND PHASE OF GROWTH

"My root was spread out by the waters, and the dew lay all night upon my branch. My glory was fresh in me, and my bow was renewed in my hand." JOB 29:19, 20

Age and experience were no guarantee against Job's decline. When deterioration sets in, it indicates a falling from a higher to a lower level, either in character, usefulness or vigor. When this happens, you are no longer the man you used to be!

Life becomes stagnant. There is a poverty in soul and spirit.

Several years ago in our nation's capital, a church leader was a guest speaker at the twenty-fifth anniversary of an organization. With an eye on the future he spoke on "The Dangers Of The Second Phase In The Growth Of An Organization." Check his five points for yourself:

1. The original revolutionary thrust of the movement tends to diminish. Status quo slowly decays the vitals of drive and persuasion.

2. There is a tendency for the ship to collect barnacles—hangers-on as well as traditions, obsolete thinking and plain old dry rot!

3. The movement or man is confronted with the problems of success. The soft and flabby middle age spread takes over.

4. The refusal to face up to failures that accompany growth; reluctance to call a mistake a mistake; afraid to lop off dead wood or useless members—the pruning of John 15 is rejected and the purifying of 1 John 1:9 is rebuffed.

5. Difficulties in transmitting the original vision to the second generation with the same enthusiasm the first generation had, arise. Older heads refuse to let go to the younger. The clay is so hardened that flexibility and mobility are gone.

Job knew the answer. Keep your roots spread out by the waters. Dryness means no fresh intake. Thomas Carlyle hit it on the head: "How did Christianity rise and spread among men? Was it institutions, organizations and well-arranged systems of mechanism? NO! It arose in the mystic deeps of man's soul; and was spread by the simple and natural individual efforts. . . . then it flew like hallowed fire, from heart to heart, till all were purified and illuminated by it.

"Here was no mechanism; man's highest attainment was accomplished dynamically, not mechanically."

To be continually refreshed and renewed keep the root system deep!

JUMPY MEN ARE NO GOOD

"My heart is troubled and restless. Waves of affliction have come upon me." JOB 30:27 (Living Bible)

A tense believer in Almighty God living on the ragged edge of his nerves is a paradox! God has not planned for His children to live all clutched up by life's problems.

Jumpy men are just no good. Ulcer candidates because of financial fears, stock market frustrations and frenzy-feelings—none of this is a realistic representation for a life settled in the providence of the Lord.

Have you known men who are so continually keyed up that it is impossible for them to relax? The pressure for sales forbids them taking a rest-filled vacation. Competitive striving and angling for advancement has taken all the thrill out of life. To rest and relax would be tragic!

Do not wait for a volcanic eruption in your emotional or nervous system. Slow down and start living the life that He has planned for you, not ceasing from work, but ceasing from your own works and from the energies of the flesh, the strivings that bring trouble and restlessness.

Dr. Clay Trumbull once wrote an article with this interesting title: "Resting Between Heart Beats." Learn the secret of spending restful and relaxing days at hard work, for the rest is not a matter of inactivity, but of being in God's will at His time and in His place.

Job needed to relax. Earlier in chapter thirty he comments, "God has placed my life in jeopardy.... I live in terror now.... My heart is broken. Depression haunts my days. . . . God has thrown me into the mud."

Inner tension and knots in the pit of the stomach are surely not of God.

Many of us at one time or another enter into this much quoted prayer: "O Lord, I am never weary of the life you have given to me, but I am often weary in it!"

Job was pointing his finger at God in his weariness. Here was a man whose sojourn was punctuated by peace, rest, and tranquility until troubles came. Then he was jumpy, tense, and nervous. Relaxing in the midst of hurricane or heartache demands the claiming of God's promises:

"Come to Me, all of you who are weary and overburdened, and I will give you rest! Put on my yoke and learn from Me. For I am gentle and humble in heart and you will find rest for your souls. For my yoke is easy and my burden is light" (Mt 11:28-30, Phillips).

NO ROOM FOR VENEER

"I made a covenant with my eyes; how then could I ogle at a girl?" JOB 31:1 (Berkeley)

Are you winning the battle in your thought life? The secret of victory is in the heart. To please God, you begin there. External conformity is not enough. You may never touch a woman, yet have an inner core that is slowly deteriorating.

Could it be that the deed of immorality was never committed because nerve or opportunity was lost? However, you still, lusted!

As with Samson of long ago, it often begins by exciting curiosity. The eye-gate has a heyday as someone new enters the field. This maiden from Timnath, Delilah, coaxed and trapped Samson. He was sucked into the vortex of sin's whirlpool. It began the day he allowed his thoughts to wander.

Spiritual bankruptcy came because he played with and egged on a tasty bit of self-indulgence. This is the concern of Job. What is just an ogle ends in adultery. Read Job 31:2-13. No room for veneer or pretense in this man's sex life.

India-paper thin is the partition between spirituality and sensuality. Find the man who is a power for God. His very strength can soon become his weakness and downfall. He may lead a double life, outwardly the Bible class leader yet inwardly a man with a fouled-up thought life.

Temptation in your thoughts is not just your peculiar affliction. Regardless of age, temperament or experience, every man is worked over by Satan in this way.

Don't treat the symptom. Hit the disease. It is pointless to get rid of crab grass by cutting off the top. Pull up the roots! Your thought life is basic.

"Only this once"—what a lie! One taste of the forbidden fruit in the Garden of Eden and man paid the eternal price for sin. One nude picture, one sexy magazine, one sensual movie, it all begins with that first one. "Our greatest security against sin is to be shocked by it."

Make a covenant with your eyes: don't court those thoughts. "I take every project prisoner to make it obey Christ." (2 Co 10:5, Moffatt).

A LEAKY INVESTMENT

"If I have put my trust in money, if my happiness depends on wealth.... For if I had done such things, it would mean that I denied the God of heaven." JOB 31:24-25 (Living Bible)

A daily ritual for tens of thousands of American businessmen is checking the stock market over the morning coffee.

They read the *Wall Street Journal* to find out what is taking place; they flip through *Nation's Business* to discover how it is being done; and they scan *Fortune* to see who's doing it all!

There is nothing wrong with all that. Just make sure that your stocks and Scriptures blend, not clash. Make sure that the points gained on the exchange board are not more important than the biblical principles by which you live. The temporal must never outweigh the eternal.

Take a good healthy look at this little story of Job, tucked away in the middle of the Old Testament. The once wealthy and influential man was bankrupt. After carefully analyzing the situation, although completely baffled by circumstances, Job asked to be weighed in the balances of moral integrity. Have I put my trust in money? Have I been depending upon wealth to assure me of personal and family happiness? If I have done this, it has been a leaky investment.

A.T.&T. is good but not good enough! More important than blue chip stock is the daily check on investments and securities for Almighty God.

Zero in on that which is worthwhile, regardless of tradition, accepted practice, or personal feelings. Many a man pours his money into that which is a purse with holes.

Examine what is being done for Christ and His kingdom around the world through the church, education, medicine, social work, and evangelism, and then after prayer and consideration—invest! Be a wise and careful steward.

Until you put yourself into God's work you will never realize a payoff. Never try to get your checkbook to do what you are unwilling to perform.

God does not need your money or stocks but He does need you. Sometimes He will strip to find out who's holding what!

"A man's harvest in life will depend entirely on what he sows.... Let us not grow tired of doing good, for, unless we throw in our hand, the ultimate harvest is assured" (Gal 6:7, 9, Phillips).

THE COST OF INVOLVEMENT

"Without making a federal case of it, God simply shatters the greatest of men, and puts others in their place."
JOB 34:24 (Living Bible)

We all want to end up where Job ended—rich in real estate, property, finances and influence with people—but most men are not willing to pay the price to get there. We want to be "proven metal" but we wholly resist the means that God uses to produce His gold. How difficult to realize that the way up is often down.

"Few men can carry great and sudden success without pride and conceit, till they are tried and humbled to carry it modestly" (Samuel Lee).

When God is making and maturing a man, note the abnormal method He uses (from man's point of view):

To set him free, there is a time of captivity.

To make him great, there is a time of being nothing.

To place him first, there is a time of being last.

To give him plenty, there is a time of famine.

To allow him life, there is a time of dying.

To assure him happiness, there is a time of affliction.

This is the cost of involvement. He shatters some men and puts others in their place. Not just to break but to build. Not just to humiliate but to honor.

I know full well how difficult it is to keep perspective. Job would encourage your heart that the highway to leadership and greatness leads through the desert trials, the lonely nights, the physical ordeals, the financial misfortunes, and always the misunderstanding of friends and loved ones.

But for God! His promises try men like Job, shattering and battering, that through the test and tribulation that man may be prepared for the fulfillment of every promise.

"Job's life is but your life and mine written in larger text. Though we may not know what trials wait on any of us, we can believe that, as the days in which Job wrestled with his bleak maladies are the only days that make him worth remembrance. So too, the days through which we struggle will be the most significant we are called on to live" (Robert Collyer).

The God who shatters the greatest of men and puts others in their place is El Shaddai, "The God sufficient for every situation."

AN ATMOSPHERE OF UNHURRIED CALM

"When He giveth quietness, who then can make trouble?"
Job 34:29

Our DC-jet had left Denver about midmorning. While cruising at 32,000 feet over Iowa, the captain reported: "Fasten your seat belts. We're beginning our descent into Chicago. Our ground speed has been 670 miles per hour!"

This is an age of speed. The race is to the swift and the battle to the strong. With a blast of hurry the world judges progress by speed and noise. Life becomes wrapped up with personal panic, noise pollution, and all types of irritations.

"The din in our homes and streets is doubling every ten years, frazzling nerves and endangering health. It's time to turn down all that noise."

How difficult it is to take time out in the midst of it all. Do you find it almost impossible to gain an atmosphere of unhurried calm? Where is the leisure and solitude that produces soul-growth? Where is that calm steadiness which belongs to those men who have confidence in God's sovereignty and timetable?

In 1692 a book was published, telling how Brother Lawrence practiced the presence of God as a monastery cook. He was never rushing nor loitering, but did each thing in its season, with an even, uninterrupted composure and tranquility of spirit.

"The time of business, does not with me differ from the time of prayer, and in the noise and clatter of my kitchen, while several persons are at the same time calling for different things, I possess God in as great tranquility as if I were upon my knees at the blessed sacrament."

That type of fruit takes time to ripen. Progress may seem so slow but do not get snagged into a maddening rush and feverish haste! We want it done "in the twinkling of an eye." God's plan is first the blade, then the ear, and then the full corn in the ear!

"Let avoidable noise be avoided. Silence is beneficial not only to sanity, nervous equilibrium, and intellectual labor, but also helps man live a life that reaches to the depth and to the heights . . . it is in silence that God's mysterious voice is best heard."

"In quietness and in confidence shall be your strength" (Is 30:15).

BE PREPARED FOR CHANGING SEASONS

"For he directs the snow, the showers, and storm to fall upon the earth. Man's work stops at such a time, so that all men everywhere may recognize His power."
JOB 37:6-7 (Living Bible)

We are familiar with the succession of the four seasons. Each has its own special characteristics. How boring would life be with just one season throughout all the year.

Consider the freshness of spring, fruitfulness of summer, harvest time of autumn and freezing of a cold winter. Just when the barrenness of winter would cause despair, out pops the new life of April! The cycle begins again!

So is the spiritual life of every man. All is not blue sky and soft warm breezes! There are the storms that baffle, failures in harvest and barren seasons that leave one stripped and cold.

Be prepared for changing seasons in the Christian life. It starts with spring: "all things are become new" (2 Co 5:17). Rebirth is a thrill, a song of renewed possibilities and a freshness that has you walking just a little bit lighter and faster.

Then comes the harsh north wind, bringing a spiritual blizzard. "Man's work stops at such a time." God has not forsaken: It is just the law of the spiritual seasons.

God's winters are not just something to be endured. Behind the storm of suffering, fear, anxiety, guilt, depression and indifference there is the sufficiency of God for such crisis days.

When the trees of your life are leafless, the ground frozen, the wheat fields brown and desolate, live by faith! God is at work! Things are happening although unseen by the human eye. This has to be in order that there will be life and growth for better years ahead.

"So that all men everywhere may recognize His power." Are you a summertime Christian, pampered by balmy breezes and palm trees swaying? God make us men who face adversity even as Job. "Though He slay me, yet will I trust in Him." Snow, showers, storm—face them as from His good hand.

Job knew that winter was to be followed by spring; darkness was only a prelude to light; pruning would make possible more fruit; and out of death comes new life!

"For it is God who is at work within you, giving you the will and the power to achieve his purpose" (Phil 2:13, Phillips).

SURRENDER OF SELF...NOT THINGS

"The Lord went on: 'Do you still want to argue with the Almighty? Or will you yield?'" JOB 40:1-2 (Living Bible)

One of man's greatest problems is not excluding God altogether, but trying to supplement Him.

God does not accept a niche in the world's hall of fame. He stands alone and unique. He is sovereign and demands undivided worship. He is all in all or not at all!

Surrender sounds heroic, romantic, chivalrous and saintlike. It may be beautiful to read about; edifying to think about; easy to talk about; entertaining to theorize about; fascinating to dream about, but believe Job, it is hard to do.

Someone must be supreme in your life. Things, interests, people and possessions beg to usurp the throne. Surrender demands the yielding of all that you are, all that you do and all that you have. Job is reminded by God that surrender is more than yielding body, family, health, habits or even his talents. Yield yourself. If God has you, He has everything.

Louis Blanc, a boastful and blatant scoffer remarked: "When I was a baby I rebelled against my mother; when I was a young boy I rebelled against my teachers; when I was a teenager, I rebelled against my father; when I reached mature years I rebelled against the government; when I die, if there is a heaven and a God, I will rebel against Him!"

"Do you still want to argue, or will you yield?" Submission always means adjustments. Rebellion begins when God puts His finger on something in your life and calls for a change, a change in attitude, a change in action, a change in deportment.

What we keep to ourselves we lose. The investment of a self-centered life yields no dividends that are satisfying or eternal.

Don't begin by giving up this or surrendering that. First of all give yourself without reservation to God. Life is tedious and conflicting when it consists of yielding on smaller issues and withholding the central core of strength.

It is one thing to be religious in spasmodic conflicts. It is quite another to hallow the entire campaign.

"O Thou Eternal, our own God, others have been ruling us; but thine authority alone today we own" (Is 26:13, Moffatt).

DON'T DESCRIBE IT—PLAY IT

"Then the Lord spoke to Job again from the whirlwind: 'Stand up like a man and brace yourself for battle.'"
JOB 40:6-7 (Living Bible)

The attractiveness of Christianity is men whose philosophy of life has blossomed into daily living, men who do not only know, but do. The vertical relationship with God is proven by a horizontal affinity with other men. Religion in the abstract is cold. Christianity in action through the life of a man of God is concrete.

You say you are that type of man. I say to you, show it! The greatest argument for your faith is a transformed life. Men want to see a working model of this "pearly gate stuff."

The daily practice of biblical principles and doctrine is what makes them attractive and believable. Without this adorning, they are merely organized religious concepts.

"Be an ornament to the doctrine of God our Saviour in all respects." Be a solid sample!

Do not repel men from the things of God because of your inconsistency. Could it be that the prodigal son left home because of the poor example of his older brother?

"Stand up like a man and brace yourself for battle." Your life speaks louder than your lips.

When is a violin most attractive? When it is played! Let Jascha Heifetz define his violin: "It is a modern treble instrument distinguished in its developed form by having the back scooped out slightly rounded like the belly, a low bridge, four strings, with curves forming the waist."

That leaves me cold! Don't describe it, Jascha. Play it!

Frigid is the religion that bickers about terms, argues about points of secondary doctrine or has bull sessions on being contemporary. Stop describing your theology. Live it!

Let God talk to you! He may not do it out of a whirlwind but what He says is most important. Stand straight and tall in the battle of life.

THE MINISTRY OF INTERCESSION

"And the Lord accepted Job's prayer on their behalf. Then, when Job prayed for his friends, the Lord restored his wealth and happiness." JOB 42:9-10 (Living Bible)

Big men for God are at their best when involved with God in the ministry of intercession.

The challenge is for you to be a channel, reaching up to God on behalf of others, becoming a mediator for men. Unlimited possibilities are available to any man who is thus occupied.

Prayer is more than asking for things. It is more than a form of pitter-patter of gushing words. Beads on a rosary or wishful dreaming about others will not do the job.

Vicarious praying, becoming a part of others' needs and their problems, is an hour for identification, not disjointed and detached. Pleading for men mirrors a selfless heart. Have you ever observed that all of Paul's prayers in the New Testament are intercessory? He lived for others and their needs.

Prayer for others rescues you from ego. Instead of looking at personal problems, aches, needs, and finances it focuses in on the campaigns and battles that others are waging.

Then, too, intercession is a deterrant. By coming boldly into the throne room of grace and pleading on the grounds of His atoning sacrifice, you can turn aside the plans of the enemy. It is not a matter of twisting God's arm nor persuading Him to do things against His will.

Know the mind of the God you are dealing with. Know Him and His promises. Persistently hang on!

Intercession is the great work of our Lord right now. "He ever liveth to make intercession." God is entreating on my behalf and for my cause. He sets the pace for sinners, sufferers and soldiers of the cross around the world.

It is on His heart. Do you have it on yours? This involvement caused Abraham to beg on behalf of Sodom and his friend Lot. It caused Moses to stand in the gap for Israel saying, "God, take my life but spare theirs."

"The warfare on all fronts and for every Christian soldier is the same warfare." Together we fight the masterful enemy. Shoulder to shoulder we stand against the loss of faith, the neglect of secret communion with Christ, the inroads of old sins. Often there appears to be no connection between our fortunes and failures and that of others, but there is an intimate, dynamic relationship.

Pray for all Christ's men.

THE QUALITY OF CALM PERSEVERANCE

"Job is an example of a man who continued to trust the Lord in sorrow; from his experiences we can see how the Lord's plan finally ended in good." JAMES 5:11

You have need of patience, the patience of Job, that quality of calm perseverance right in the teeth of the angry blast, riding out the storm undisturbed.

When the Sabeans stole Job's cattle and oxen, when an act of God wiped out his sheep, and the Chaldeans stole his camels, Job had to be patient. The ancient cattleman from the land of Uz might have expressed his masculine constancy under trial in this fashion: "The purpose of my life is to make me what the Almighty wants me to be. Then I shall not measure things by their capacity to delight and please my tastes, ambitions, desires and senses, but only by their power to mold me in His likeness."

More enterprises and noble causes are ruined through lack of patience than through lack of skill, knowledge or energy. When we lose patience we lose faith in God, in ourselves and in others. Impatience begets discouragement, driving a man alternately to ill-considered activity or deadening apathy.

The teacher is God. The subject is patience. The lesson illustration is from the life of Job. Here are a few points from the lecture:

1. Patience is the endurance of suffering without giving way nor giving in to self-centered feelings of paying back for injuries incurred.

2. Patience is fortitude under great seige of trial without losing heart and courage.

3. Patience is an attribute of God, developed and nurtured in the mill of experiences where the grinding is exceedingly slow.

4. Patience is the full consent of a yielded will, never allowing disappointments, grief, heartaches or loss to become an excuse to sulk, shirk, or sin in ungodly impatience!

People cause us to be short-tempered. When irritating circumstances arise, we simmer, sizzle, scorch and steam up a stew! Such fluctuations should drive us to a more constant consideration of the All-Patient One.

Consider Jesus Christ who endured name calling, spittings, jestings and total rejection. Deserted by His loved ones, mocked by his enemies, stripped of all human dignity by the masses, "yet He opened not His mouth." Lest ye be wearied and faint, allow Him to become your patience pacesetter!

Part 2

A CHALLENGE FROM PSALMS

when the ceiling is zero

Psalms is more than just a challenge from the heart of man to men. It represents the heart of God to hearts of His men. It has very appropriately been labeled, "a handbook for personal devotions." Here is heart encouragement for men burdened by trouble and anxiety. It might also be titled "Personal Peace amid a Disturbed World."

This compilation of one hundred and fifty poems has both a devotional and a prophetic theme for practical living. The thoughts presented are not new. They are reminders of old truths.

Read the devotional meditation first and then after a short prayer for guidance and wisdom, read the psalm directly from your Bible. Perhaps one of the modern translations will shed new light on old and favorite paths. Beware of a challenge without application. Follow through with whatever God is speaking to you about.

BE LIKE A TREE

"Blessed is the man . . . he shall be like a tree". PSALM 1:1, 3

Tertullian was reprimanding a neighbor accused of shady practices in business. The fellow defended himself, "But a man has got to live."

Tertullian answered, "Why?" To Tertullian it was more important to be a man of principle than to make a good living.

This first psalm is a thumbnail sketch of a truly happy (blessed) man. The rest of the book tells us how to live and enjoy this unique life of overflow.

A godly man of principle is a happy man. Note the contrasts in this chapter between the one man in ten thousand and the fellow who is intrinsically worthless. One is happy and fortunate, the other is unhappy and miserable. The righteous is like a tree, the wicked is like chaff. Tertullian's man is fruitful and flourishing, his neighbor is empty, unserviceable and full of vanity. God's man has a solid foundation, the other is swept away by folly.

The contrast is sharp and in focus. The choice is inevitable and we all must make it. Which man will you be?

Be known by the company you avoid! This is negative purity but it is a pathway you must follow. Definite prohibitions, absolute renunciation, unchanging laws of spiritual declension are necessary. "It is a sign of inward grace when the outward walk is changed."

Be known by the things you love! This is the positive pursuit. Here is a man who gets excited about the Holy Scriptures. They are not a bore nor a drag but, "How sweet are Thy words unto my taste! Yea, sweeter than honey to my mouth!"

Be known by what you are! A man can hate sin and love righteousness because he is grounded and fixed. He can do something because he is something. He can bear fruit because he has a root system. He does not "run out of gas" because he is always within reach of an unfailing supply.

Have you ever met a man who prospered, flourished and looked like a huge success only to come into his forties and fifties with decay and disaster? He probably never answered Tertullian's question "Why?" He probably never incorporated this first psalm into his life's philosophy. Be a man who is planted like a tree! Be a man who is prosperous, perennially young, vigorous and fresh. Be a man who has the guarantee of permanence, "his leaf also shall not wither."

TAKE TIME OUT

"Salvation belongeth unto the Lord: thy blessing is upon thy people. Selah" PSALM 3:8

Following the Civil War there were scattered across the western part of the United States a multitude of stagecoach stops to break up a difficult trip for rest, relaxation, and refreshment.

This is the meaning of the Hebrew word *Selah,* stop and rest or reflect awhile. Take time out to catch your spiritual breath and reorganize the loose ends of your thinking. Most men realize their need for a Selah; but, in the midst of a busy and full life, few know how to come to this complete stop, unbend, and give the matter at hand undivided attention.

Selah appears seventy-one times in strategic places in the book of Psalms. It gets the attention of the reader so that he will slow down and not miss the message. Selah marks a pause for inventory, investigation and involvement. Starting with Psalm 3:2, take time out to look up every outcropping of this fascinating little road sign. Stop! Look! Listen!

The opinion of some is that Selah is a musical rest note, a musical pause while the singers relax and meditate on what they have just been chanting. Other men feel that Selah is a note of exclamation. The lyrics hit such a responsive note that one must stop and burst out in praise. Read the third chapter of Psalms; and when you come to Selah, instead of repeating this word, say, "Think of that!"

Another possibility is that Selah could mean a change in pitch, a musical sign to indicate to the singers and orchestra that they should rise to a higher key. Psalm 3:2 is minor and doleful. Then Selah is inserted and things are different. Clouds give way to sunlight in verse three! Listen to it: "There is no help for him in God. Selah. But thou, O Lord, art a shield for me; my glory, and the lifter up of mine head."

A higher level is reached. Selah in the Hebrew is what excelsior is in the Latin: "Higher." Get up!

The pile driver can only work when it is pulled up high and allowed to drop with more bounce. The committed life in Christ is that higher life. Lift the strain, sing more loudly, pitch the tune on a higher key. Across the barren plains of your life today, stop! Take a good look at the past. Learn its lessons and with cheerful anticipation look into tomorrow.

"Every morning tell him, 'Thank you for your kindness,' and every evening rejoice in all his faithfulness" (Ps 92:2, Living Bible).

REMEMBER THE MORNING WATCH

"My voice shalt thou hear in the morning, O Lord; in the morning will I direct my prayer unto thee, and will look up."
PSALM 5:3

The intimacy of communion with Christ must be recaptured in the early morning quiet time.

The year was 1882 when on the campus of Cambridge University the Christian world was first given the slogan: Remember the Morning Watch.

Students like Hooper and Thornton found their days crowded with studies, games, bull sessions, visits and speakers. Enthusiasm and activity was the order of the day. These dedicated men soon discovered a flaw in their spiritual armor, a small crack. If not soon closed it would bring disaster.

They sought for an answer and came up with the Morning Watch, the plan of spending the first half hour or the first hour of the day alone with God in prayer and study of the Bible.

The idea caught fire. A remarkable period of religious blessing followed, that culminated in the departure of the Cambridge Seven for missionary service, that band of prominent athletes and men of wealth and education who gave up everything to go out to China for Christ.

But these fellows found that getting out of bed in time for the Morning Watch was as difficult as it was vital. Thornton was determined to turn indolence into discipline of desire. He invented an automatic foolproof cure of laziness.

"The vibration of an alarm clock set fishing tackle in motion, and the sheets, clipped to the line, moved swiftly into the air off the sleeper's body." Where there's a will, there's a way!

Activity for Christ and time alone with Christ go hand-in-glove.

Not because others are doing it, not as a spiritless duty, nor as an end in itself, but guard, nourish and maintain your daily Morning Watch for what it means. Practice the presence of God in devotions, leading to a steady walk with Him throughout the day.

"Cause me to hear thy lovingkindness in the morning; for in thee do I trust: cause me to know the way wherein I should walk; for I lift up my soul unto thee" (Ps 143:8).

PRACTICE GOD'S PRESENCE

"I have set the Lord always before me." PSALM 16:8

Life is affected by the things you see day by day. Men living in gloom develop a gloomy outlook. Fellows who live in the world of mathematical figures can easily degenerate into calculating IBM machines.

If that which you see is bigger and better, it rebukes your littleness and badness. A lesson we all need to relearn continually is that the presence of our Lord makes the difference.

The story is told of a burglar, rifling a room, who caught sight of a small bust of the Lord Jesus. As he prowled about, it seemed to be watching him from the mantle. The mere sight of it so disturbed his conscience that he went over and turned the carving's face toward the wall.

Consciousness of God's continual presence is indispensable. Success in anything is only reached by a steady and consistent view. "All of us . . . because we continue to reflect like mirrors the splendor of the Lord, are being transformed into likeness to Him" (2 Co 3:18, Williams). Changed by beholding.

It was cool that day in the garden when God came to fellowship with Adam and Eve. They were disturbed in their conscience and had hidden themselves behind a bush. Where could they flee from His face? To the rising of the sun, or the faraway places of the ocean they knew, "Thou God seest me."

The doctrine of Christ's presence lies at the foundation of Christian faith. The more you are persuaded of the fact of God's continual presence, the more victorious will be your daily experience.

Beware of locating the presence of God in a wafer upon some church altar. Never be satisfied with a substitute when your deepest need is the awareness of the reality of His presence.

Brother Lawrence was a lay worker employed in the kitchen of a French monastery during the seventeenth century. Amidst the noise and clatter of his pots and pans, he was attuned to God's nearness. It was here in the routine that he penned the recommendation, "Practice the presence of God."

"He leads me in paths of righteousness for His name's sake. Yes, though I walk through the valley of the shadow of death, I will fear no harm; for Thou art with me" (Ps 23:3-4, Berkeley).

FULLNESS OF JOY

"Thou wilt shew me the path of life: in thy presence is fulness of joy; at Thy right hand there are pleasures for evermore."
PSALM 16:11

"I want to be happy. I want the moon, or the sun, or something." So wrote Robert Louis Stevenson to one of his friends.

Life that is so attractive that it soon becomes contagious and infectious is the desire of most men. The sour, gloomy and melancholy professing Christian is a poor advertisement.

How tragic to discover behind the gusto, big smile and happy disposition that the proverb is ever so true: "Even in laughter the heart is sorrowful; and the end of that mirth is heaviness" (Pr 14:13).

Joy is far more than a burst of pep or a side-stitching belly laugh.

The Bible speaks in terms of joy and rejoicing, but shies away from the term happiness. Joy is the fruit that results from life lived in the presence of God. Happiness depends on good circumstances.

Life can become a frenzied quest for some new sensation, a persistent thirst for pleasure. The glum, depressed and morbid disposition is not of God. He lays the foundation for a built-in drive for satisfaction.

In your loneliness and sorrow, God gives songs in the night. Paul and Silas in jail rocked the inner dungeon at midnight with their singing. This visiting gospel team had joy, not just happiness. They were "making melody in their hearts to the Lord" (Eph 5:19).

"Joy has a tonic effect. The early disciples were irrepressible. They departed from judgment halls with bleeding backs, rejoicing that they were counted worthy to suffer for His name. They rejoiced their way through prisons, and saluted death with a smile. The fruit of the Spirit, joy, kept their souls above the storm and strife."

Do not be satisfied with the mere tinsel of happiness when the pure gold of joy is yours for the asking.

"Rejoice in the Lord alway: and again I say, Rejoice" (Phil 4:4).

A PERSONAL RELATIONSHIP

"The Lord is my shepherd; I shall not want." PSALM 23:1

Here is one of those biblical statements that scratches where most men itch! It is ointment for many a modern burn.

The truth of the first five words is not so much questioned as is the relevancy of the statement.

The climate of our changing times is a good cause to crack open Psalm 23:1 and examine the contents. Follow along with me.

To place any other name in this statement in place of the Lord would never work. Even the greatest in history would fall far short. Try it! As an illustration try "Abraham Lincoln is my shepherd; I shall not want." It will not work. Neither will father, nor mother, nor pastor. And who is the Lord that can be such a shepherd that I shall never want? Jehovah God is His name. The creator, the sustainer, the maintainer, the counselor, the Lord God of Abraham, Isaac and Jacob. He is the same Shepherd of John 10 Who states: "He goes in front of them himself, and the sheep follow him because they know his voice" (v. 4, Phillips).

"The Lord *is* my shepherd." There is no if, nor but, nor I hope so; nothing in the past tense nor the dream possibilities of the future. It is a relationship of now. He has been, He will be, but best of all, He is right now. God is not just the historical leader of the Jewish people. He is contemporary with the latest moment.

If He be a shepherd to no one else, He is a shepherd to me! He is not just a shepherd of a nation, nor of a generation, nor of the world, but of individuals. This takes it out of the realm of generalities and makes it specific. There may be ninety-nine others in the flock, but I am that one lost lamb that He cares enough about to seek and save!

Let the farmer say, "My crops shall keep me, I'll not want." Let the businessman say, "My stocks and securities will do." Let the soldier say, "My weapons will guard me, I have no fear." Let the educator say, "My books and wisdom will be sufficient to meet my needs." How empty, how futile, how shallow compared with the man who says, "The Lord is my shepherd; I shall not want." Crops, stocks, weapons, books—these can never feed, guard, guide, govern and love you as does the good Shepherd.

"My sheep recognize my voice, and I know them, . . . they follow me. I give them eternal life" (Jn 10:27-28, Living Bible).

HAUNTED BY HAZARDS

"I sought the Lord, and he heard me, and delivered me from all my fears." PSALM 34:4

What is the antidote to fear? Is it to keep a stiff upper lip, keep whistling, keep smiling and everything will come out all right?

Multitudes today are haunted by hazards. Fear makes a man a coward. Fear makes a fellow cringe and say, "I cannot." Success becomes impossible. The spirit is killed.

Panic can be caused by the real and the imaginary. A man who fears the internal is pathetic. He whose fears are external lives in despair.

Fear is like an enveloping fog which clouds a man's vision; like a cold, chilly hand upon the heart.

Every day throughout the world millions of men experience fear!

At a critical time of his life, D. L. Moody made his confession concerning the proposition of fear. He stated that he had learned to take his stand upon the Rock, and rejoiced in the fact that in spite of storm, temptation or darkness, he was still standing firm. He quoted the remark of an Irishman who said: "I tremble sometimes, but the Rock never does."

To the Christian, fear is the direct opposite of faith. "Faith is the assurance of the things we hope for, the proof of the reality of the things we cannot see" (Heb 11:1, Williams).

Faith is the belief that God is present. His promises are trustworthy. He has proven Himself in meeting and overcoming the fearing heart. Thus, there is nothing to fear.

Unbelief minimizes God by magnifying difficulties, producing fear.

"Fear is shattering the nerves of multitudes. Fear paralyzes the hands and hearts of men engaged in work of great importance. Fear drives valuable men from their positions of responsibility to seek the counsel of a doctor or psychologist. Fear dogs a man's steps and hounds him during the night."

"For God hath not given us the spirit of fear; but of power, and of love, and of a sound mind" (2 Ti 1:7).

OUR WRISTWATCH—GOD'S TIMETABLE

"Delight thyself also in the Lord; and he shall give thee the desires of thine heart. Commit thy way unto the Lord; trust also in him; and he shall bring it to pass." PSALM 37:4-5

Commit your way unto God. Roll it onto him. Leave to Him the right to call the strokes of your life. Turning points in big and little decisions allow you to develop the habit of committing your steps to God.

Reliance on God is not a cowardly way of shifting the problem onto another. Nor is it a lazy way of begging life's decisions. God does not side-step man's common sense, judgment or brains. These are second. His will is first. Our wishes and plans are to be subordinated to Him.

The committed way of simple and unwavering trust suggests burning all your bridges behind you and surrendering everything to God, a definite act of faith.

Begin by being convinced that the Word of God is utterly reliable and He is prepared to guard that which we commit to Him.

"I know whom I have believed, and am persuaded that he is able to keep that which I have committed unto him against that day" (2 Ti 1:12).

Continue by daily trusting Him. Never hand over to Him that which a few hours or days later you take back. Some will commit their way to the Lord, but find it mighty difficult to maintain this attitude of commitment on a day-by-day basis.

Finally, wait for Him to bring it to pass. Here is the age-old conflict between our wristwatch and God's timetable. Like little boys wanting a red fire engine for Christmas, we just cannot wait to possess our coveted request.

God is never before His time and never is behind. Commit—trust—wait!

"God gives His very best to those who leave the choice with Him."

THE SECRET OF BACKING OFF

"Be still, and know that I am God." PSALM 46:10

When all else fails, try reading the instructions!

In your drive to get ahead, to lead the pack, to forge to the front, have you missed the force that makes life different? Impact and power do not come from jamming the accelerator of your life to the floorboards, nor from forming a new committee with the intended bureaucratic purpose of doing something.

Try reading the instructions of this marvelous psalm. No wonder it has gone down in history as "The Song of Holy Confidence." It is probably remembered best as Martin Luther's Psalm, for no matter what happened, Luther would read this song and come out happy and secure.

Be still. Get quiet for a short period of time. Perhaps you find yourself living in the loud, noisy, slam-bang world described by Dr. Sam Shoemaker:

"The pace is excitingly fast. Everywhere is great scientific achievement. There is fear in every sensitive heart . . . there is want of satisfying emotions, increase of unreason, rebellion, loss of regard of personality, easy dismissal of the spiritual as irrelevant.

"Most men live in quiet desperation . . . gnawing loneliness, and vague, intense bitterness, besides the eternal fact that success and security come not from haste and hurry . . . but from quietness and stillness."

Perhaps the words of George Santayana were never more true: "Fanaticism is redoubling your efforts when you have forgotten your aim!"

Look back over your shoulder at the time consuming pressures of recent weeks, the pursuit for position, the drive for money and power, the thirst for security and satisfaction. Has it been worth it all?

The power of stillness comes as you are willing to withdraw and disengage yourself from much of life's barren busyness.

"Take time out. Give God time to catch up with you and speak. Give yourself time to be silent and quiet before Him, waiting to receive, through the Holy Spirit, the assurance of His presence with you. His power working in you. Take time. You'll never have it till you take it" (*The Secret of Adoration*, Andrew Murray).

PLAYBOYS STILL GET BURNED

"Wash me thoroughly from mine iniquity, and cleanse me from my sin." PSALM 51:2

Experimental sex for human fulfillment is not new morality. It has been around for at least three thousand years. A story similar to the tale of David and Bathsheba in 1 Samuel 11:1-5 happens every day.

What is rare today is a confession like David's.

Sexual stealing used to be taboo. The twentieth century has accepted and approved "free love." Playboys still get burned, but are commended for not being puritanical squares.

David was a man of strong passion. He got what he wanted over the back fence. But an aroused conscience caused him to cry out and confess his guilt. We remember his sin but the Holy Bible dwells on his repentance.

Many a man curses the day he gets caught but could care less about his crime. Not so David, he was broken by his adulterous sin. David was sick of the transgression, not just the tough consequences. Bathsheba's husband was willfully killed, the illegitimate baby died, the kingdom was divided, and David lost his right to build a temple. But to him, the worst part was that he had sinned against God.

"What I did not think shame to commit, that let me not think shame to confess" (John Baillie).

This formula still works today! Psalm 51 is rightly called the sinner's guide. Those men that come God's way find His mercy and grace for every stain.

"He that covereth his sins shall not prosper: but whoso confesseth and forsaketh them shall have mercy" (Pr 28:13).

UP TO YOUR NECK IN TROUBLE?

"Cast your burden on the Lord, and He will sustain you: He will never allow the righteous to be pushed over."
PSALM 55:22 (Berkeley)

What do you do when the load gets too heavy?

Have you ever tried running away in hopes that a change of circumstances would ease the weight?

Some would recommend a stiff upper lip, muddling through somehow.

But how about those times that David expresses: "For problems far too big for me to solve are piled higher than my head. . . . My heart quails within me" (Ps 40:12, Living Bible)?

God will never allow you to be loaded with a greater burden than you can bear. He is faithful to come to your rescue. You can always count on Him.

What should you do when the load gets too heavy? Cast it on the Lord. He is the burden bearer, the load lifter, the comforter and the undergirder.

This burden that we are commanded to cast upon the Lord is a Hebrew word that literally means "the portion assigned to thee." It is that which God in His gracious supervision feels to be your allotment:

It may be the treachery of a trusted friend, the load of financial pressure, the heavy burden of inequality, the tragedy of a child who sows to the wind and soon is to reap the whirlwind.

Are you faced with the burden of ill health, unemployment, misunderstandings, crippling anxieties, some sharp thorn of sorrow that you cannot share with another living soul?

He has not promised to remove the burden but He always sustains! He has promised, "My grace is sufficient for thee: for my strength is made perfect in weakness" (2 Co 12:9).

"Let him have all your worries and cares, for he is always thinking about you and watching everything that concerns you" (1 Pe 5:7, Living Bible).

GET STARTED TODAY IN PRAYER

"If I regard wickedness in my heart, the Lord will not hear; but certainly God has heard; He has given heed to the voice of my prayer." PSALM 66:18-19 (NASB)

Aha Farh Whart Innevin Hollow Beety Name . . .

Surely this is not pig latin, nor could it possibly be German! It is the opening phrase of the Lord's Prayer as spoken by the man who is rushing to get through. Say it, and be gone. It is purely the chanting of sounds that have no meaning.

The pitter-patter of pompous platitudes does not make prayer. Big words, loud shoutings, meaningless Amens and hallelujahs can easily be pretense with no reality. They sound great, but so does a parrot in a wind tunnel.

Posture does not make prayer. Men have communed with God while standing, kneeling, sitting, lying down, walking on water, tossing in a whale and hanging from the cross. The position of the body is not paramount.

Prayer does not rely upon location, but the Scripture does encourage us to seek a place without distraction. "When you pray, go into your room, shut your door and pray to your Father privately. Your Father who sees all private things will reward you" (Mt 6:6, Phillips).

Purpose to pray. Get started today, not in theory, but in action! You do not need more knowledge to pray, you need practice. You may have the talent, but God is interested in production. Plan your attack.

Prepare your heart for prayer. The words of your mouth and the meditations of your heart must come from an altar that is clean, purified and holy. Preparation takes time.

Persevere in prayer. Hold on tight in faith believing.

"'Call to Me, and I will answer you, and I will tell you great and mighty things, which you do not know.'" (Jer 33:3, NASB).

QUALITY OF GUILELESSNESS

"May it never happen that those who seek Thee, be brought to dishonor on my account." PSALM 69:6 (Berkeley)

Do you put into practice on Monday morning what you so religiously profess on Sunday?

The trap of inconsistent living is always underfoot. In Psalm 69 David is lamenting the curse of being such a stumbling block to his fellowmen. It is bad enough, he states, to be hated and misunderstood without cause or justification. How much more tragic when there is a cause. "May it never happen" that there is an ill-advised remark, a heated temper, a careless action or an indifferent attitude causing a friend or neighbor to be "ashamed through me."

Men may not understand our doctrine and theology but they are observing our practice around the clock. They are anxious to see if a Christian is a producer or merely a professor!

Saint Peter knew well the need for a behavior and manner of life that was steady seven days out of the week. At his conversion he received a new life, a new center of values. He allowed God entrance into every area of his life. Eight times Peter uses in his biblical letter a word translated "wholeness."

Not long ago, two business associates were chatting about a mutual friend, a man who started in a blaze of glory and suddenly flopped with one fantastic bang!

"How did it happen?" one friend asked.

"He had everything but what he needed," the other man answered.

Needed today are men who shape up to the pattern of Christ, men who are not tattered and frayed around their moral edges. How may a Christian have this quality of consistent guilelessness?

That kind of life can come only through God's provision through the enabling of the Holy Spirit.

"He has by his own action given us everything that is necessary for living the truly good life" (2 Pe 1:3, Phillips).

BEAR WITH OTHERS, PLEASE!

"But he, being full of compassion, forgave their iniquity, and destroyed them not: yea, many a time turned he his anger away, and did not stir up all his wrath. For he remembered that they were but flesh." PSALM 78:38-39

The size of a man is measured by his tolerance. This is an important mark of maturity in a day of racial discrimination, religious bias and class distinctions.

Evangelist Jonah was so parochial that there was no slack in his spiritual cable. When called to go evangelize Nineveh, he headed in the opposite direction. Because the Ninevites were not God's chosen people, bigoted Jonah had no concern for them.

Tolerance causes a fellow to bend, allows him to see that he is not the whole, only a part. Differences must not sever and divide but in a spirit of understanding and consideration; "In lowliness of mind let each esteem other better than themselves" (Phil 2:3).

The mechanic allows for minute play in the engine; the state highway patrol gives a warning ticket; the baseball catcher drops the foul third strike and the batter gets new life. This is tolerance!

With God we call it mercy and longsuffering. The All-gracious One is never too rigid nor bound by rules and regulations that He cannot bear up His creation. This is demonstrated in the story of the wilderness wanderings of the children of Israel.

They were released from Egypt by a miracle. They were fed with water from the rock and manna from heaven. Their clothes did not wear out and they were protected continually. "Nevertheless they did flatter Him with their mouth, and they lied unto Him with their tongues. For their heart was not right with Him, neither were they stedfast in His covenant" (Ps 78:36-37).

Think of how amazingly others tolerate you. Bear with others, please!

"Why, then, criticize your brother's actions, why try to make him look small? We shall all be judged one day, not by each other's standards or even our own, but by the judgment of God" (Ro 14:10, Phillips).

A MAN'S SUCCESS STORY

"Teach us to number our days and recognize how few they are; help us to spend them as we should."
                                    PSALM 90:12 (Living Bible)

When you see a well-organized, planned and productive life, you can rest assured that it is no accident.

There are one hundred and sixty-eight hours a week to spend or to gamble. A wise man has set up an investment portfolio for his time. He guards it with resolution, handles it with precision, and invests it with acumen.

A fruitful, happy and holy life consists of fruitful, happy, and holy days. These days are made up of fruitful, happy, and holy moments! They are not produced by chance. They are the habit, desire, and conviction of men who walk with God.

So thought a religious leader of the seventeenth century, Horatius Bonar. After seeing the failure in his personal life and ministry, he incorporated the following resolutions:

1. "In imitation of Christ and His apostles, and to get good done, I purpose to rise timely every morning."

2. "To prepare as soon as I am up some work to be done, and how and when to do it; to engage my heart to it; and at even to call myself to account and to mourn over my failings."

3. "To spend a sufficient portion of time every day in prayer, reading of the Holy Scriptures and other profitable spiritual exercises."

4. "I will spend once every week four hours over and above my daily portion in private, for some special causes relating either to myself or others."

5. "To spend some time on Saturday, towards night, for preparation for the Sabbath."

This is a man's success story. Through self-discipline and godly purpose he had learned to use time wisely.

Are you caught in a time squeeze? Do you feel harassed, swamped, and pressured? This prayer of Moses is a challenge for each man: "Teach us to number . . . help us to spend."

Of all the rules in arithmetic, this is the hardest: "number our days." We know the acreage of our lands, the books tell us the amount of money in the bank, the payroll ledger keeps us abreast of our employees and yet our most valuable asset, time, is flying away.

"Be very careful, then, how you live. Don't be unwise but wise. And make the most of your opportunities because these are evil days" (Eph 5:15-16, Beck).

PROBLEMS TOO BIG TO HANDLE?

"When my anxious thoughts multiply within me, Thy consolations delight my soul." PSALM 94:19 (NASB)

Here is the story of man's extremity and God's opportunity.

The psalmist was a deeply afflicted man. As he was tossed to and fro in his thought life, he made the supreme discovery of the only harbor of safety and peace, the consolation of the Lord. Kicked around with problems, distractions, questionings, forebodings, and fears, he discovered that God's promises were not only a comfort, but a delight.

Dr. Charles Bradley has stated the case so beautifully: "In the nature of the consolations . . . being comforts . . . there is tranquility; in the number of the consolations . . . there is sufficiency; in the owner of them . . . God . . . there is omnipotency; and in the effect of them . . . there is security!"

Observe the greatness of the psalmist's problem. The word translated "cares" originally meant the small branches of a tree. "The arms of the tree shoot out in every direction, entangling and entwining themselves one with another; let the wind take them . . . see how they feel it, how restless they become and confused, beating against and striving one with another. Man's mind is like that storm beaten tree. Thoughts and cares which are continually shifting and changing; they are perplexed and agitated thoughts, unbelieving, despondent, worldly, repentant . . . all battling one with another. There is no keeping the mind quiet under them . . . they bring disorder as well as sorrow, perplexity as well as oppression, pressures as well as tumult!"

What are the possibilities for deliverance?

Just in time and with the proper application the consolations of God come charging in to take control. Both in the perplexity as well as the plurality of problems, God is the answer! "The reward I get from the Lord Jesus Christ, from looking at Him, from considering Him, from thinking about His Person, His office, blood, righteousness, intercession and Coming Again . . . this is the anchorage and stabilizer I must possess."

What are you doing with your problems? Covering them? Running from them? Blaming them on others? Try God's way!

"What a wonderful God we have—he is the Father of our Lord Jesus Christ, the source of every mercy, and the one who so wonderfully comforts and strengthens us in our hardships and trials" (2 Co 1:3-4, Living Bible).

THE DISCOURAGEMENT OF LONELINESS

"I am like a pelican of the wilderness: I am like an owl of the desert. I watch, and am as a sparrow alone upon the house top." PSALM 102:6-7

The solitude of loneliness is a frightful situation for many.

Loneliness often will bring along discouragement, downheartedness and despair. How these roll in like an ocean fog completely engulfing the soul and spirit.

A void has been created that must be filled. Do you remember the story in the Bible, following the crucifixion of Jesus Christ, when His followers were feeling mighty low and droopy? Their leadership was gone, their cause seemed lost and they decided to go fishing in a weak attempt to fill the emptiness.

But emptiness cannot be filled with a fishing trip, a good book or a stiff drink.

Note that the geographical place often contributes to the attitude—the wilderness, the desert, the house top. In such barren places, it seems that there is no one to hear, to help. Yet, the Christian has the assurance that he is never completely alone.

When all seems lost and no one really cares the "Friend that sticketh closer than a brother" makes His presence felt. Alone? The Maker of time assures you, "Lo, I am with you always."

To feel alone is not the same as to be alone. The facts remain. God is there just as much as He was with Elijah in the wilderness or the disciples down by the Sea of Galilee.

Consider David during one of his lonely hours. He felt like a pelican, an owl, a sparrow! These birds specialize in solitude.

Consider Jacob during one of his lonely hours. He was more than circumstantially alone. He was lonely. Things had gone from bad to worse. He was so low there was just one way to look and that was up! "And Jacob was left alone . . . and God blessed him there" (Gen 32:24-29).

It is not the mere fact of being a pelican, an owl or a sparrow that is blessed, not just being alone with ourselves in fruitless introspection. It is being alone with God!

"Two are better than one; because they have a good reward for their labour. For if they fall, the one will lift up his fellow: but woe to him that is alone when he falleth; for he hath not another to help him up" (Ec 4:9-10).

TAKEN FOR GRANTED

"Bless the Lord, O my soul, And forget none of his benefits."
Psalm 103:2 (Berkeley)

How easy it becomes to take things for granted. All of life's extras become expected and we become irritated when some of the extras do not come our way.

Commonplace is the sunrise, beautiful spring weather, singing birds, splendid health, faithful friends, our nation with all its security and happiness. We catalogue many blessings as downright ordinary, run-of-the-mill routines. How about stopping long enough to thank God for breathing, seeing, hearing and the ability to think clearly?

Life is so loaded with benefits that we become spoiled. Are we a generation who have lost the thrill for the simple? "The Lord's lovingkindnesses indeed never cease, For His compassions never fail. They are new every morning; Great is Thy faithfulness" (Lam 3:22-23, NASB).

Today, have you noticed the beauty of God's creation?

Have you noticed today how others have served you, prepared your meals, cleaned your clothes, provided your electricity, heat, running water and the daily paper? The barber, the bus driver, the baker and the banker may go unnoticed until their services are missed.

Have you noticed today men in need with empty stomachs, aching hearts, broken bodies and frustrated purposes? With nations tottering and Christless millions around the world dying without God's love, have your eyes lost their perspective in a cold stare of self-centeredness?

Have you noticed today God's hand of mercy, His heart of love, His grace to forgive?

Remember all His benefits! Pause and praise Him.

"What return shall I make to the Lord for all His bounties to me?" (Ps 116:12, Berkeley).

THEY GOT WHAT THEY WANTED—BUT

"And He gave them their request; but sent leanness into their soul." PSALM 106:15

The children of Israel had emerged from Egypt by way of the thrilling Passover night, the dramatic Red Sea deliverance, water out of a rock in the desert, yet they kept pestering Jehovah for meat rather than miracle food called manna.

The people were enthusiastic about their destination but dull about the route that God had chosen. They loved their new-found freedom but certainly not their food. Their prayers became fleshly, selfish, materialistic, and ego-centered. These men were not willing to wait for God's will but were not to have their own.

The high cost of low living—they got what they wanted and were cursed with the burden of answered prayer. Better for them if God had said no. But God gave them what they wanted.

Their flesh was fat and their spiritual life became empty. The outer man won but the inner man lost.

Lot prayed for the fertile valley and the soft life. He got what he asked for plus the curse of Sodom and Gomorrah. Esau wanted something so badly he could taste it:

"Watch out that no one becomes involved in sexual sin or becomes careless about God as Esau did: he traded his rights as the oldest son for a single meal. And afterwards, when he wanted those rights back again, it was too late, even though he wept bitter tears of repentance" (Heb 12:16-17, Living Bible).

There does not have to be this sting to every lovely thing. Right praying means happy living. Stop asking for the safe and easy life that ends in sorrow and sin. Gilt-edged security takes away from trusting God for each day's needs.

"Be delighted with the Lord. Then he will give you all your heart's desires" (Ps 37:4, Living Bible).

TWENTY-FOUR HOUR SECURITY GUARD

"He shall not be afraid of evil tidings: his heart is fixed, trusting in the Lord. His heart is established, he shall not be afraid." PSALM 112:7-8

Have you ever doubled up your fist and exclaimed, "I am not going to be afraid?"

This is the psalmist's personal affirmation. Here was a man who was hunted, chased, condemned, accused and battered. He often had to change his plans but never the purpose of his heart.

The heart that is fixed or established has the idea of being prepared and ready. That which is able to meet every situation, ready to stand its ground. In the Hebrew language the word *fixed* carries with it three basic ideas.

It gives the idea of firmness. The Hebrews used it when they wanted to speak of the most utterly immovable thing their minds could conceive. It gives the idea of preparedness, as one who is seasoned, conditioned and matured. Finally, the word *fixed* carries the thought of serenity, unruffled calm even in the heat of battle.

Job is a terrific illustration of a holy heart that gives a brave face. Bad news and evil tidings had struck hard. All was lost. Job had put his confidence in God, therefore his heart was kept in amazing poise. "The Lord gave, and the Lord hath taken away; blessed be the name of the Lord" (Job 1:21).

His heart is fixed. Consider Moses before the Egyptians; Joshua facing the murmuring Jews; Jehoshaphat before the horde of Ammonite invaders; King Asa encountering the Ethiopian's "thousands of thousands, and three hundred chariots."

His heart is established. Consider Daniel and his three buddies in their impossible circumstances; consider Stephen before the religious council that was dedicated to his death; consider the apostle Paul who faced everything from tribulation to famine, from nakedness to the sword!

The secret of it all is trust in the Lord. He alone is the source of confidence and help. God is our twenty-four hour security guard.

The next time you double your fist to say you will not be afraid, remember this as you do it. Take your little finger first: "He shall not be afraid." Next, your ring finger: "His heart is fixed." Now your middle finger: "He shall not be afraid." Then your pointer finger: "His heart is established." Now tie it all together with your thumb. Double up your fist as your thumb locks the grip of your hand on God, affirming as it falls into place: "Trusting in the Lord."

OPERATE ON THE CANCER

"I thought on my ways, and turned my feet unto thy testimonies. I made haste, and delayed not to keep thy commandments." PSALM 119:59-60

A desperate situation demands drastic measures! Never is this more pointed than when deterioration sets in. How tragic to see a promising young life wasted. What a tragedy is lost potential.

There is danger ahead when you observe the crumbling and cracking of basic foundation stones. Remember Samson. When he wanted most to exercise his God-given power, it was already deteriorated.

The rusting of his resistance caused a flabbiness to soften his entire life and testimony. Ability and desire to say "no" went out the window with deterioration. "He wist not that the Lord was departed from him" (Judg 16:20).

One of the damning causes is carelessness in upkeep. Neglect brings in decay. "I went by the field of the slothful, and by the vineyard of the man void of understanding; And, lo, it was all grown over with thorns, and nettles had covered the face thereof, and the stone wall thereof was broken down" (Pr 24:30-31).

Daily, consistently, with life-saving vigilance prevent the weathering of time from eroding away at your assets, your blessings, and your causes. Seek His strength to resist temptations that make you careless, fightless, and Godless!

Discover the damage and enact some drastic measures. Operate on the cancer that eats away at your life. If you have been placed in the moth ball fleet, scrape off the barnacles and paint. Repent! He will restore.

God's vocabulary is picturesque and plain. The rotting process is called backsliding. Only His blood can cleanse and renew!

"So tighten your loosening grip and steady your wavering hand. Don't wander away from the path but forge steadily onward. On the right path the limping foot recovers strength and does not collapse" (Heb 12:12-13, Phillips).

STAKE A CLAIM—START TO DIG

"Thy word is a lamp unto my feet, and a light unto my path."
PSALM 119:105

In every fellow there is just enough boy to love a good treasure hunt.

Vast fortunes wait to be discovered at the bottom of the sea. Treasures are hidden on some lonely isle. Men dream of a storehouse of gold as told in the legends of the Southwest Indians. Suppose you find a faded note with simple instructions leading to this wealth. By simple obedience, if this letter tells the truth, you can become a rich man.

In the same way, if you will take the Lord at His word and follow the instructions given in Scripture, you will discover hidden treasures.

The Bible is not a human book, but divine. It is not just clever reporting on the part of ancient Jews, it is the revelation of the heart of God as "Men of God spoke because they were inspired by the Holy Spirit" (2 Pe 1:21).

It is not just the book of the month or the book of the year, but the Book of the Ages. It is never outdated, old-fashioned or useless.

Lost? Here is the perfect guide. Sick? The remedy from the prescription pad of the Great Physician. Confused? Confidence and assurance bulge from every page of Holy Writ.

This is your challenge to join in the great gold rush. Stake a claim and start to dig. You will find a rich vein.

The treasure is food for the hungry, nourishment for the babe in Christ, vitamins for the spiritually weak. Eat all you can daily!

It is a mirror! Take a good long look at the dirty garbage of the human heart. Take an even longer gaze at the cleansing fount of Calvary. Do not smash the mirror, you cannot change your looks that way!

The treasure is a lamp, giving light for guidance and illumination. A blind man does not need light, he needs to have his eyes opened. Then he can see the light.

It is a seed! Likened unto a time bomb ticking away in your heart, ready to explode you into a man after God's own heart. Let this seed fall into the good, soft, open soil of your heart.

Go gold digging with God! Pioneer today into every deposit. Explore the Bible!

"Every young man who listens to me and obeys my instructions will be given wisdom and good sense. Yes, if you want better insight and discernment, and are searching for them as you would for lost money or hidden treasure, then wisdom will be given you and knowledge of God himself; you will soon learn the importance of reverence for the Lord and of trusting him" (Pr 2:1-5, Living Bible).

DOMINATED BY COSTLY STANDARDS

"Therefore I esteem all thy precepts concerning all things to be right; and I hate every false way." PSALM 119:128

Greatly needed in every walk of life is a standard of conduct which will serve as a guide for straight living.

This is an hour when men are diseased with laziness, short cuts, complacency and that consuming desire for the fast buck. Where are the high standards of excellency and models of morality that have been the backbone of generations past?

"Why work hard and long? Victorian is the concept that cheating and lying is sin. Do what is expedient" is like dry rot eating away the basic timbers of a man's character.

When in Rome, do as the Romans do, a moral erosion that has cut through man, leaving gaping holes of standardless existence.

Internal standards condition what a man is. The intent of the heart determines the moral character of the act.

The Ten Commandments (God's standard of behavior) were put in the negative for they can only restrain man's actions. They cannot implant positive integrity and moral excellence. Statutory standards can apply the brakes and regulate actions, but they cannot transform the wayward heart!

Daniel was dominated by costly standards. His personal habits, his behavior before king and servant, his relationship to money, position and attainment, all these served as a tonic for his generation. His standards before man and God brought a nation to that fine edge of moral conviction that makes greatness.

"Daniel distinguished himself, because of his surpassing spirit. . . . he was faithful, and no error or fault was found in him" (Dan 6:3-4, Berkeley).

Raise your sights. Start living on that higher plane made possible by Holy Scripture and the Holy Spirit.

OPTICAL RECONNAISSANCE

"The unfolding of Thy words gives light; It gives understanding to the simple. I opened my mouth wide and panted, For I longed for Thy commandments."
                              PSALM 119:130-131 (NASB)

Three doctors, specialists at a medical school, went into the hospital wards for some case illustrations for their lectures.

One was a psychiatrist. He found a patient suffering from a severe nervous breakdown. One was a skin specialist. He found a woman suffering from a bad skin disease. One was an expert on stomach and digestive troubles. He found a patient with persistent diarrhea.

No one noticed that the object lesson used by all three of the great specialists was the same woman, until an old country doctor, a general practitioner, glanced at her case history and cried: "Dementia, dermatitis, diarrhea. Why, this woman has pellagra!"

And he was right. The specialists saw the symptoms, but the country doctor knew the disease.

How often we go by looking at the seemingly obvious and completely miss the heart of the matter. This is a challenge for optical reconnaissance of basic issues. Do not be derailed by fleeting and fascinating side issues.

So often a man's background conditions his vision. The economist sees the world's problems in terms of supply and demand. The sociologist sees symptoms of suffering, hints of hunger, heartaches of war. Politicians, historians, military strategists—each sees what he is looking for from his perspective. Schopenhauer said, "Every man takes the limits of his own field of vision for the limits of the world."

As you open your Bible, what are you looking for? Do you seek confirmation of a pet doctrine, verses that will seemingly stamp God's approval on your self-made plans, or, as David prayed, "Open thou mine eyes, that I may behold wondrous things out of Thy law" (Ps 119:18).

WORSHIP CANNOT BE BY PROXY

"I was glad when they said unto me, Let us go into the house of the Lord." PSALM 122:1

One of our great American heritages is the freedom to commune with God according to the dictates of individual hearts.

When the Lord Jesus Christ sought the most intimate communion with His Father, He got alone. The assembled disciples were left behind, not just for the purpose of isolation from people, but for single-hearted devotion to God.

Your new birth relationship in Christ demands expression without reservation.

This worship cannot be by proxy. Other men may know God only by His works. You can know Him by His ways before He acts. Psalm 103:7 is the proof. You have the privilege of meeting Him in a personal quiet time daily. You have the responsibility to meet Him in communal worship.

Do not limit your fellowship just to the Lord's Day. But do not forsake the fellowship of the local church. Receive the benefit of united prayer, cooperative worship, and togetherness in service!

Public worship gives you the opportunity to witness of your faith in Christ. A deaf man faithfully attended his church. He could not hear anything. Someone finally asked him why he bothered to go.

"I want my neighbors to know whose side I'm on."

It may be possible to be a Christian and not belong to a church, or ever attend one. But it is not wise or pleasant. "For none of us liveth to himself" (Ro 14:7).

"Live unto the Lord exclusively. Look unto the Lord believingly. Sing unto the Lord gratefully. Give unto the Lord generously. Hearken unto the Lord obediently. Pray unto the Lord continually. Serve unto the Lord reverently."

"For where two or three are gathered together in my name, there am I in the midst of them" (Mt 18:20).

STRONG, STABLE AND SECURE

"They that trust in the Lord shall be as Mount Zion, which cannot be removed, but abideth forever." PSALM 125:1

Those who fully trust in Jehovah become distinguished by their unmovable qualities.

They possess an even keel when the storms are severe. They have the capacity to stand tall when adversity strikes. They enjoy a security when the blast hits head-on.

"Wisdom and knowledge shall be the stability of thy times" (Is 33:6).

W. H. Page would remind us that some men are like sand, ever shifting and sliding. Some are like the sea, restless and unsettled. Some are like the wind, uncertain and inconstant. Others are as a flower, weak, seasonal and temporal. But the God-fearing man is like Mt. Zion, strong, stable and secure.

Is there any possibility of Pikes Peak being removed? Impossible! How about Everest, McKinley or the Rock of Gibraltar being shaken and removed?

Absurd! Note that this verse does not state: "May not . . . will not . . . nor shall not." Neither by force from without nor fickleness from within, the man who trusts in God is like Mt .Zion and *cannot* be shaken.

Man may lose his money, his health, his family or his friends, but he cannot be removed! You may lose the fellowship, and the communion but you cannot be removed "from God's heart of love, nor out of His covenant grace which is sure and everlasting. You may lose lands but not the Lord, nor from off His heart, nor from off Him as your foundation" (John Gill).

So take courage. Believe God! You shall be just as He says: "All who listen to my instructions and follow them are wise, like a man who builds his house on solid rock. Though the rain comes in torrents, and the floods rise and the storm winds beat against his house, it won't collapse, for it is built on rock" (Mt 7:24-25, Living Bible).

TEARS OF THE MANLY

"He who goes forth weeping, carrying seed for sowing, shall doubtless come again with joy, carrying his sheaves."
                                             PSALM 126:6 (Berkeley)

Some have associated religion with the hysteria-shrieks of a pennant-waving teenager at the ball game.

"If you must be religious, play it cool," they counsel. You are branded immature if you are emotionally involved in your relationship with God. The modern advice is: "Use your head. Harness your heart."

I beg to differ. There is nothing more offensive than a dehydrated Christianity. Life without emotions would be blah!

"By starving emotions we become humorless, rigid and stereotyped; by repressing them we become literal, reformatory and holier-than-thou. Encouraged, emotions perfume life; discouraged, they poison it."

Emotionalism apart from the working of God in a deep spiritual experience is to be shunned. However, the lack of "tears" in the heart and eyes of most men could be a signpost of a cold heart, unbroken spirit and unrepenting will.

True tears are the sign of brokenness. The removal of hardness and resistance by a sensitivity to sin is the heart of Godly religion.

How easily we become hard, proud, "intellectually balanced" and soul dry. Are you afraid of showing, enjoying or emotionally expressing your faith in the Living God?

Be like the farmer. In the spring he cries with the sowing of the grain. He is tired of plowing, exhausted from walking the fields, wearied as he has planted the crop. Tears are the exterior evidence that he feels deeply.

But wait till harvest! The thrill of waving grain, the joy of putting in the sickle, shouts of praise as the granary is loaded are the recompense for his labor.

Take courage. Heaviness will turn to harvest. The toil of labor will be rewarded with God's pay check. Tears now? Joy will soon be here!

"Let us not grow tired of doing good, for, unless we throw in our hand, the ultimate harvest is assured" (Gal 6:9, Phillips).

ACKNOWLEDGE THE GIVER

"Except the Lord build the house, they labour in vain that build it: except the Lord keep the city, the watchman waketh but in vain." PSALM 127:1

Success in itself is not an evil; but the more you succeed, the more you need to watch and pray. Each aspect of success has its own peculiar danger: power, of suffocating in your own importance; wealth, of tripping over your own greenbacks; fame, of being blinded by the glittering approval of others.

The higher the rung on the ladder of success, the rarer the atmosphere. Giddiness may set in and cause you to use your power, privileges, and personality for exploiting rather than for blessing others less fortunate. And the people on whose fingers you trod while climbing up are the very ones you will have to pass on the way down!

But the greatest danger is *self*—self-centeredness, self-importance, self-confidence, self-reliance. "Why call on God? *I* can easily take care of that little matter." Self takes over and leaves God out.

Nebuchadnezzar, king of Babylon, had reached the top; and the whole earth lay in his power. "Is not this great Babylon, that I have built for the house of the kingdom by the might of my power, and for the honour of my majesty?" (Dan 4:30). So he thought! But God had a lesson to teach him "that the most High ruleth in the kingdom of men, and giveth it to whomsoever he will" (4:25).

Demented, Nebuchadnezzar lost his throne, was driven from society, and lived like a wild beast in the fields, until God restored both his mind and authority. Humbled, he acknowledged "the King of heaven, all whose works are truth, and his way judgment: and those that walk in pride he is able to abase" (4:37).

Whatever rung you have reached in your climb to success, acknowledge the One who has enabled you to do so. Trust Him to keep you there, and use your position to His glory.

SPEND TIME WITH A RISEN SAVIOUR

"Search me, O God, and know my heart: try me, and know my thoughts." PSALM 139:23

Would you say your attitude is good or just untested?

It is possible to have an acceptable disposition and temperament, yet through lack of conflict and challenge even you may not be sure of your attitude when the chips are down. How do you react when you do not have the time to think and prepare?

The twelve men of the Master were not proven. But under the shadow of Calvary, their basic heart attitudes were revealed.

Judas sold out for a cheap price.

Peter blatantly denied Christ. The enemy's fire warmed his body but froze his heart.

Asleep in the Garden of Gethsemane were the three indifferent disciples. While the Son of God was taking up the sins of the world, these lads were unconcerned and ignorant.

Yes, the disciples at first appeared deflated and defeated yet two months later they emerged invincible! What was the secret of this new-found success? They spent time with a risen Saviour! Luke reports, "Did not our hearts glow within us while He was talking to us on the road and opened the Scriptures to us?"

A faith that became a bulwark to withstand the surge of circumstances made impact. Bitterness, annoyances, apathy and ruffled attitudes were supplanted by joy, peace, and humility.

Now it was not what they held but what held them. They had been grasped, laid hold of, conquered.

"But the people who know their God shall be strong and do great things" (Dan 11:32, Living Bible).

ONENESS GETS THE JOB DONE

"How wonderful it is, how pleasant, when brothers live in harmony!" PSALM 133:1 (Living Bible)

Without contradiction, the impact of unity is great.

Whether it be in your business, on the ball field, or in the army, oneness gets the job done. Concord replaces competition, riveted together rather than rivals against.

Unity is more than being one hundred per cent agreed in opinions, verbal assent to religion or even cooperation in practice. It cannot be artificial, man-made, or cooked up in a religious chem lab.

It is not a manufactured product. Unity is a result of heart relationship, a united front on the inner level. God makes unity. Our job is to keep it. He is our bond. We are glued together in the Lord.

"Continuing with eager earnestness to maintain the unity" (Eph 4:3, Williams). Faith unites, doubt divides. Doctrine builds, strife whittles down. Love blends, jealousy splits.

Communism seeks to drive wedges between liberty-loving people. The enemy's tool is one of dissection.

According to David in this psalm, harmony is likened unto "fragrant anointing oil" and "as refreshing as the dew." Togetherness smells good, feels good and starts your day off with an invigorating challenge.

Where is the oil and dew today among men? Pride and selfish interests find fellows pitted against each other. There is too much spiritual and emotional babyhood among grown men!

United men in a manifesto for Christ is the absolute necessity of our day.

Start today with the one man you can influence most—yourself!

"Your hearts beating in unison, your minds set on one purpose . . . in humility practice treating one another as your superiors. Stop looking after your own interests only but practice looking out for the interests of others too" (Phil 2:2-4, Williams).

TASTE YOUR WORDS

"Set a watch, O Lord, before my mouth; keep the door of my lips." PSALM 141:3

"But I tell you that for every careless word spoken men shall be answerable in the Judgment Day" (Mt 12:36, Berkeley).

Careless, useless words do no work and have no profit.

Speech is an index of character. How often at the corner drugstore, over a cup of coffee in the office or casual relaxation in the neighbor's living room, unguarded talk betrays the real man!

Watch the heart, for it is the fountain. "Out of the abundance of the heart the mouth speaketh" (Mt 12:34).

Random talk reveals far more than deliberate speech.

Idle words, "words which are physically transcient, but morally permanent . . . cannot be undone; they are spoken without profit to speaker or hearer."

This kind of chatter is insipid and tasteless. "Let your speech always be gracious and so well reasoned out that you will know how to reply to each individual" (Col 4:6, Berkeley).

How little attention we pay to our tongue. How seldom we taste our own words. The current thinking seems to be that if we do right it matters little what we say!

The spirit of levity and a sense of humor easily become a form of self expression and a fleshy trait. Light talk, undisciplined joking, and jesting—this is not a part of the framework surrounding a man of quality and depth.

Surely this does not apply to humor, conversation and day-by-day chatter that helps to lighten life's burdens. Christ is dealing with a principle, not condemning communications in general.

An unbridled tongue has been referred to as "the chariot of the devil." Do you pray about the jokes you tell? Are you prepared to give account for every conversation? Hand the reins of your lips over to the Lord. Guard the door of your mouth.

"Keep your mouth closed and you'll stay out of trouble" (Pr 21:23, Living Bible).

Part 3

A CHALLENGE FROM PROVERBS

when the ceiling is zero

Proverbs is a book for every man in everyday circumstances. Ethics, economics, politics, home life, business, morality and the tongue are only some of the many topics it covers.

Proverbs is a collection of maxims woven into a didactic Hebrew poem around the general topic of wisdom. The form of Hebrew poetry is not based on the repetition of similar sounds, but on a repetition of ideas which complement or contrast each other. This is called parallelism.

As you are moving through Proverbs, substitute the name of Jesus Christ whenever you come to the word wisdom. "But of him are ye in Christ Jesus, who of God is made unto us wisdom, and righteousness, and sanctification, and redemption" (1 Co 1:30).

FREEDOM FROM GUILT

"But the one listening to me will dwell secure, will be quiet without dread of calamity." PROVERBS 1:33 (Berkeley)

Most men live within the framework of a respectable guilt complex. Outwardly they may seem serene and calm but within is unrest and self-chastening.

Instead of dwelling securely, men dread failure and misbehavior. Christians may experience guilt feelings for spending time in private and public devotions and not enough time with the children, or for giving more money to the church when the family bills are not paid, or for spending hours reading theological books until they can no longer carry on a decent conversation with their business associates on current events or sports.

But if that same person were to reverse his behavior he would still be caught in the bewildering labyrinth of guilt. He would chasten himself for neglecting devotions, robbing the Lord, and neglecting his Christian education in favor of secular subjects. Where does it end? What can be done?

First of all, be thankful for your conscience. It was given to you by Almighty God. Then remember, through the sacrificial blood of Jesus Christ, all guilt has been removed. If you simply confess it all to Him, the slate is wiped clean. Keep your eyes on Him, not man. Follow His rules, not man's.

Here are some suggestions that might be of help:

1. Never do anything you are in doubt about.
2. Never do what you know is wrong.
3. Do everything you know to be right.
4. Put everything aright you have done wrong, as far as possible.

Keep short accounts with God and man.

"Make sure that your conscience is perfectly clear, so that if men should speak slanderously of you as rogues they may come to feel ashamed of themselves for libelling your good Christian behavior" (1 Pe 3:16, Phillips).

WELL ALL RIGHT—DIG, DIG!

"If thou seekest her as silver, and searchest for her as for hid treasures; Then shalt thou understand the fear of the Lord, and find the knowledge of God." PROVERBS 2:4-5

God's treasures are not lying on the surface for easy pickings. The man who would know his God and Bible must be one who is willing to dig. And we all know that digging is hard work. It takes time, energy, diligence, and concentrated attention.

Note the verbs of manly action in the first few verses of this second chapter of Proverbs: receive, hide, incline, apply, cry, lift, seek, search." All of these are involved in Bible digging.

The Bereans of Acts 17:11 are a good example of this. They "studied the Scriptures every day to see if what they were now being told were true." (Phillips) How about that Old Testament character, Ezra? "For Ezra had disciplined himself to study the Law of the Lord" (Ez 7:10, Berkeley). Needed are men with the cultivation of discipline in digging. More men should devote themselves to searching the scriptures.

Nathaniel Shaler tells about studying under the famous Swiss scientist Agassiz. "Dr. Agassiz brought me a small fish, placing it before me in a tin pan with the rather stern requirement that I should study it, but should on no account talk to anyone concerning it nor read anything relating to fish until I had his permission to do so.

"In the course of an hour I thought I had compassed that fish; it was rather an unsavory object, giving forth the stench of old alcohol, and I was anxious to get on to the next stage of training. But Agassiz, always within call, concerned himself no further with me that day nor the next nor for an entire week! It was indeed distressing for I had sat before that 'stinking' fish for over 100 hours.

"I finally set about to work upon the thing . . . how the scales went in series, their shape, the form and placement of the teeth, etc. I now felt confident and so when the Doctor asked for my discovery, I was amazed at his answer: 'That is not right, try again.' After another week of ten-hours-a-day labor I had results which astonished myself and satisfied him. I shall never forget the sense of power which this experience brought to me.

"I had learned the art of comparing objects. I now began to appreciate my instructor's advice: Look, look, look!" King Solomon's advice to each of us would be the same: Dig, dig, dig!

GUIDEPOSTS FOR GUIDANCE

"In all thy ways acknowledge him, and he shall direct thy paths." PROVERBS 3:6

"The stops of a good man, as well as his steps, are ordered by the Lord," said George Muller of Bristol, England. God opens some doors, and closes others. Both are means that the Almighty God uses in guiding His own.

Never forget that a guide must be reliable to be of service. He must have credentials as to his capacity and reliability. For pilgrims and strangers, guidance is an imperative necessity. We have the need. God knows the way.

We need guidance as to what to say and how to say it. We need guidance as we tend to the affairs of business life. Husband and wife need direction as they strive together to make their home a gracious habitation for family and guests.

One of the great chapters of the Bible is the Twenty-third Psalm. Notice how this masterpiece starts off: "The Lord is my Shepherd; I shall not want. He maketh me to lie down in green pastures; He leadeth me." The place to begin in every area of your life is to allow Him to call the strokes. Let God be sovereign in your affairs. Crown Him, then He shall direct your paths!

James H. McConkey gives us several guideposts to observe as we seek to know His will and then do it. First of all, there is no royal road to guidance. It is taught only in God's school. All the following factors are used to direct your life: prayer, Holy Scriptures, personal temperament, advice from friends, submission, patience and a total "leaning not on your own understanding."

Another great clarifier in guidance is waiting! Time allows for secondary sediments to deposit at the bottom. Trifling things assume their proper place of insignificance. Big things loom up in proper importance. "Haste is more often a trap of Satan than it is a necessity of guidance." "He that believeth shall not make haste" (Is 28:16).

Guidance is usually a step at a time. We want the blueprint spelled out far in advance. This is faith's severest test and faith's highest development. Are you willing to live just for today? Just for this hour? Moment by moment?

Finally, guidance is usually cumulative. "God forges one link after another in the chain of guidance until the whole is complete and convincing." He gives joy and blessing for what He is leading us into and distaste and unrest in what He is leading us from. Union of many factors and heart responses are pretty sure proof that "This is the way, walk ye in it."

GUARD YOUR HEART

"Above all that you guard, watch over your heart, for out of it are the sources of life." PROVERBS 4:23 (Berkeley)

It is easy to find out what is inside a jug. Just tip it over and pour. What is inside is what comes out.

So it is with men. "Out of the abundance of the heart the mouth speaketh," said the Lord Jesus. "A good man out of the good treasure of the heart bringeth forth good things: and an evil man out of the evil treasure bringeth forth evil things" (Mt 12:34-35). It is a good test to use on your acquaintances: what makes up most of their conversation—encouragement, praise, cheerfulness, and truth, or gossip, bickering, lying, and profanity?

But, beware! The same test can be used on you by them.

Have you tried to guard your mouth? Your efforts may have been effective temporarily; but, sooner or later, there is a slip. That little tongue within is like a fire, untamable, and full of poison, as described in the epistle of James.

What about your heart? There is the real source of thoughts and deeds as well as words. But again Scripture warns: "The heart is deceitful above all things, and desperately wicked: who can know it?" (Jer 17:9).

Self-reformation is not sufficient. It is like washing the outside of the jug and relabeling it: changing the label on the outside does not change what comes out.

But do not give up. There is hope and help in God. He searches the heart and shines in to give the light of the knowledge of Him (2 Co 4:6). Commit yourself—mouth, heart, and all—to His keeping.

"Search me, O God, and know my heart: try me, and know my thoughts: and see if there be any wicked way in me, and lead me in the way everlasting" (Ps 139:23-24).

LASSO, LARIAT, LANYARD

"His own iniquities seize the wicked, and he is held fast by the ropes of his own sin." PROVERBS 5:22 (Berkeley)

The scissors of self-effort can never do the job of releasing a man who is caught in the trap of his own making. Like a wild beast of the jungle, the rebellious life is captured and held prisoner by unyielding ropes. Habits grip. Evil deeds become evil habits. Do it once and it is much easier to do again. It is as hard for the Ethiopian to change his skin or the leopard his spots as for those men who are accustomed to do evil, now to do good.

Remember the time you said, "I'll only do this once." Now you are imprisoned in a firm clutch, and if you were to tell the truth, the power to resist is just about gone.

Impulses increase as motives decrease. Many a man is so wrapped in the net of evil deeds that he commits the sin once more, not because he finds any pleasure in it, but for no better reason than that he has committed it so often the habit of doing it is his master. Like an octopus, "the ropes of his own sin" drag a man down and down.

Proverbs was written to warn men of the cords that the enemy would use to incapacitate and deaden their testimony and influence. The lasso of lust, the lariat of laziness, and the lanyard of loose ethics are well described by Solomon.

Note some of the monuments of catastrophe in the Bible when great men got their feet, hands, hearts and souls so entangled with the ropes of sin that they (apart from the grace of God) were left writhing and paralyzed in utter uselessness.

"I will go out . . . and shake myself," said Samson the judge of Israel. But he could not. The chains that were at first made of mere grass and silk, now were formed of iron and steel. It was on the lap of a sinful woman that the threads of the cable were being weaved day by day until it could not be broken.

King Saul was consumed by jealousy, envy and pride until he died on the battlefield by his own sword.

Esau was caught in the cords of fleshly desires, Elijah by the cords of discouragement, Jeremiah and his ropes of despondency, Demas by the lure of success, and Judas by the web of stealing.

The cords can be loosened and shattered! Take heart! The ministry of Christ was to sinful man. He was anointed to preach deliverance to the captives.

AN EXCELLENT TEACHER—THE ANT

"Go to the ant, thou sluggard, consider her ways and be wise."
                                                                PROVERBS 6:6

September is the time for children and young people to go back to school. How often as parents we will be heard to say: "Learn your lessons well!"

We need to go back to school ourselves and learn some basic lessons of life from the tiny ant. Man is big but amazingly dumb. The ant is little but exceedingly wise. Be humble enough to be taught from one of the Creator's smallest object lessons, the ant.

Three important lessons can be learned from the tiny ant.

First of all, be wise in foresight. "The ants are a people not strong, yet they prepare their meat in the summer" (Pr 30:25). If there is going to be a spending time, there must be a gathering time. If I intend to harvest, I surely must sow. An enjoyable winter is based upon a summer of hard work. Prepare in plenty for times of need; provide in time for eternity; lay the foundation in life for death. Only the foolish man lives like the grasshopper, singing, idling and empty-hearted. When winter comes he dies while the ant is abundantly cared for. Work while you can. There is coming a day when you will not be able.

Learn from the ant to be wise in organization. According to Proverbs 6:7 these little ants have "no guide, overseer, or ruler," but, my, how they turn out the work. They live and work together, nest and share their food. The ants of a colony never quarrel among themselves, continually pulling together; and one thing for sure, there is no bureaucracy to bother with!

There is a third lesson to be learned from the ant. Be wise in industry. Ants are always on the lookout for food. They constantly are caring for the queen ant, feeding her, guarding her from enemies, digging new tunnels and rooms for new ants and more food. All the day long they are busy, busy, busy! No wonder the ant is one of God's favorites. He always loves the hard worker. Well it has been said the two men that God will never use are the lazy and the coward. Learn from the ant for it is neither.

In this day of ease, idleness, slothfulness and indifference, may this be a challenge to learn from the ants and be wise.

LIVING IN THE SEX SET

"My son, keep my words . . . that they may keep thee from the strange woman." PROVERBS 7:1, 5

This chapter tells the tragic story of wearing a white suit down into a dark and dirty coal mine! This is a warning to men against the lusts of the flesh.

Solomon, remembering what had happened to his father David, knowing the tendencies of his own feeble heart, watching the addiction of his own sons, does all he can to shout out warnings concerning the dangers of playing with the fire of adultery.

Take a look at the tempted man as he is described in chapter seven. He is a young man, void of understanding surrounding purity and mixed up with a crowd of "simple ones." Immature, untaught, and unprotected he becomes easy prey! Note another problem, he had no plans for the evening hours.

Take a look at the woman doing the tempting. She is married but unfaithful, sexily dressed, crafty in her approach, talkative and self-willed, externally religious and internally rotten!

Beginning with verse thirteen is the temptation and its seeming success. Never is sexual temptation greater than when it seems to be innocent, enjoyable, unknown to others, and justifiable.

Verses twenty-two and twenty-three tell of this man "shot down in passionate flames." As an ox, as a fool, as a bird! As an ox, he thinks he is going to feast in green pastures, and all the while he is being led to the slaughter house! As a fool, he thinks he is going to play and have a great time, and all the while he is being chained in the correction stocks! As a bird, he thinks he is going to eat some easy food, and all the while he is being caught in the teeth of the trap!

Those who succumb to the temptation become like department store merchandise: "slightly soiled—greatly reduced in price."

The best defense against the lust of the flesh is a good offense in the Word of God: "Keep, lay up, bind, and write them upon the tables of the heart."

> This Book will keep you from sin:
> Sin will keep you from this Book.

THE POWER OF NEGATIVE THINKING

"Reprove not a scorner, lest he hate thee: rebuke a wise man, and he will love thee. PROVERBS 9:8

The Power of Negative Thinking might never become a best seller at the local bookstore, but it is surely solid biblical counsel.

To accentuate the positive and eliminate the negative is the philosophy of many religious faddists. "No" has just about disappeared from the average home, school and working situation.

"No" is a bad word that springs from a diseased mind, or so they tell us. "Thou shalt not" was for the good old days but it is outdated for the twentieth century.

A great, big booming "NO" is just what is needed for this anemic and spineless day. We need to emphasize biblical negatives, not just some self-strutting negativism. "Chasten thy son while there is hope, and let not thy soul spare for his crying" (Pr 19:18). The Garden of Eden clearly heard the big "no" from God, and the Ten Commandments major on negatives!

The book of Psalms begins with this negative: "Blessed is the man that walketh not, standeth not, sitteth not." Note the sermon that Jesus Christ preached from the mountain. It is loaded with "don'ts." "Do not your alms before men, when ye fast, be not, as the hypocrites, lay not up for yourselves treasures upon earth, ye cannot serve God and mammon, judge not, that ye be not judged."

God needs men who cannot only take a no but also say no. Walk close to the Lord, close enough that you can hear Him when He is saying no to you. But remember that when He says, "No, not that way," He shows you the way you should go.

"Trust in the Lord with all your heart and lean not on your own understanding. . . . Be not wise in your own eyes" (Pr 3:5, 7, Berkeley).

SATISFACTION OR INCOMPLETION?

"As vinegar to the teeth, and as smoke to the eyes, so is the sluggard to them that send him." PROVERBS 10:26

Are you a man who calculates the cost so you can deliver the goods, a man who finds a great satisfaction in life from finishing what is begun? Inconsistent jacks-of-all-trades do not really enjoy life. Life at its best is found in completing a deal, signing the contract, crossing the goal line.

Men who putter around listlessly trying this and that find that they accomplish little and life is a bore. God has built into most men an inner happiness that breeds from completing one thing after another, like the gratification that welled up in the heart of St. Paul, "I have run . . . I have fought . . . I have finished."

Could it be that you are a man who can really stir up the dust of activity, but is long gone when it starts to settle? How sad it would be if a bronze tablet is erected in memory to your life: "Ardently begun—completion date permanently postponed!"

When you are given the ball, do not stop, hesitate or drop it. Run for the goal line! Do you leave things unfinished because you have lost interest or became discouraged? With a multitude of attractions, it is easy to become dazzled by other things so that concentration and consummation become dissipated.

Of all the excuses rendered for not putting on the finishing stroke to a project, perhaps the greatest of all is this: there was no intent to finish, even at the beginning. A useful person is faithful to the very end.

"No one who puts his hand to the plough, and then continues to look back, is fitted for service in the kingdom of God" (Lk 9:62, Williams).

THE FLUCTUATIONS OF FINANCES

"He that trusteth in his riches shall fall: but the righteous shall flourish as a branch." PROVERBS 11:28

Few things are so much at the mercy of life's fluctuations as money.

What can money do for you? It does not satisfy. The wealthier one becomes, the more money he wants.

Millionaires who laugh heartily are rare!

"What then are they doing if they are not laughing? They are carrying burdens which crush all laughter out of them. They are carrying the thing which promised to carry them" (J. H. Jowett).

In 1923, a very important meeting was held at the Edgewater Beach Hotel in Chicago. Attending this meeting were nine of the world's most successful financiers. Those present were:

the president of the largest independent steel company;
the president of the largest utility company;
the president of the largest gas company;
a great wheat speculator;
the president of the New York Stock Exchange;
a member of the President's Cabinet;
the greatest "bear" in Wall Street;
head of the world's greatest monopoly; and
president of the bank of International Settlements.

These men had found the secret of making money. Twenty-five years later their situations had changed.

Charles Schwab lived on borrowed money and died a bankrupt;
Samuel Insull died a fugitive from justice and penniless;
Howard Hopson was found insane;
Arthur Cutten died abroad insolvent;
Richard Whitney was released from prison;
Albert Fall was pardoned from prison so he could die at home;
Jesse Livermore died a suicide;
Ivar Krueger died a suicide; and
Leon Fraser died a suicide!

All these men learned well the art of making money, but not one of them had learned how to live.

"Lo, this is the man that made not God his strength; but trusted in the abundance of his riches, and strengthened himself in his wickedness" (Ps 52:7).

STERLING DURABILITY

"A man shall not be established by wickedness: but the root of the righteous shall not be moved." PROVERBS 12:3

The wonders of the ancient world numbered seven. They were great in size, unequaled in beauty, breathtaking in design and skill of construction, but only the pyramids remain. The rest are gone, deteriorated and leveled. Somehow they lacked the sterling quality of durability. The man-made wonders flunked the test of time by crumbling and falling apart at the seams.

These wonders cause a man to stop and wonder what ingredients go into durability. What does it take to outlive, outgrow and outlast? A man possessed by the Creator should be as solid as the Rock of Gibraltar.

In sight of the victor's wreath, Solomon stubbed his toe and became a magnificent flop, not for lack of coaching, rule book, or spectator encouragement. With a great splash in the mud, the author of Proverbs became a bungler in the basics.

Compromise in marriage caused Solomon's meteoric collapse (1 Ki 11:1). "When you run in double harness, take a good look at the other horse."

Then, too, worldly success spoiled him. He took first-rate interest in second-rate issues.

He wilted under heat, melting like butter instead of standing pat. Persistent Paul challenged the first-century men: "So, my brothers beloved, stand firm, immovable, always abounding in work" (1 Co 15:58).

"So you must take on God's full armor, so as to be able to take a stand in the day when evil attacks you, and after having completely finished the contest . . . hold your own. Hold your position" (Eph 6:13-14, Williams).

GOD HATES IT

"Only by pride cometh contention: but with the well advised is wisdom" PROVERBS 13:10

Mark it down on your memory pad that whenever you are at odds with someone else, pride is heavily involved. Pride makes you impatient when someone contradicts you in opinion or personal desire. Competition and rivalry are outcroppings of pride. Quarreling over rights and anything that resembles a slight could be proof positive that you are downright proud!

Pride makes a god of self. Pride overevaluates abilities, superiority and accomplishments. You may be proud of race, face, place, and even grace! Pride covets praise and caters to applause. It deeply desires and schemes to be in the limelight.

Contention is guaranteed with pride. What used to a beautiful friendship can be ruined. This happens in families, neighborhoods, governments, and, tragic but true, it seems to be paramount in the church. Pride causes trouble in board meetings, PTA elections, Bible classes, financial hassels in the home, or perhaps the terms of a business contract.

Paul and Barnabas were earnest Christians and outstanding church ambassadors. "The contention was so sharp between them, that they departed asunder one from the other" (Ac 15:39). Both of them were good Christian men who could not live and work happily together.

Pride sows hatred among the brethren, and God hates it.

What is the wisdom of the well advised? Humbly ask God to reveal the black, hidden serpent of pride. In the light of His holiness ask for cleansing from outbreaks of temper, uncharitable judgments, impatience and stubborn self-will. Recognize the differences between men in character and outlook, remember each has his place in the body. Apply Romans 12:18 today! "If it be possible, as much as lieth in you, live peaceably with all men."

THE GOLDEN OX

"Where no oxen are, the crib is clean: but much increase is by the strength of the ox." PROVERBS 14:4

To have a harvest, there must be hard work. Before the use of machinery, this meant a team of oxen. No oxen? Then there will be no chores, no feeding, no manure to haul, no yoke to repair, and no plow to sharpen! Twenty-four hours a day you could be proud of a clean barn since there was no reason to get it dirty.

But never forget the other side of the picture. Where there are no oxen, there will be no harvest. No harvest means no money, and that means no food. How can a man have a crop without the care of oxen? It cannot be done!

The success story of any farmer consists of long hours, hard work, heartaches and blisters, plus the care of oxen.

This divine principle is simple. Get rid of the means of production, oxen, and you cut your work load down to nil. The crib will be clean and there will be no manure to haul, but there will be no profits either.

We complain about leanness when we should be concerned about laziness. Don't get bogged down in details, routines, secondaries, "means to the end," and the machinery. All these are necessary, but they are only the oxen. We are not working for the ox. He is working for us!

Lean Christianity so often looks at the work in the barn and has no vision to see down the months to fruit in the field. Digging into Scripture, fervency in prayer, laboring for the hearts of men, and the daily exercise of being about your Father's business; these are the golden oxen that make for a bountiful life.

"If a man will not work, he shall not eat." Now we hear that you have some among you living quite undisciplined lives, never doing a stroke of work. . . . Our order to such men . . . settle down to work and eat the food they have earned themselves. And the rest of you—don't get tired of honest work!" (2 Th 3:10-13, Phillips).

SEEK WISE GUIDANCE

"For lack of advice plans go wrong, but with many counselors they are accomplished." PROVERBS 15:22 (Berkeley)

Some men think they have all the answers to problems, business situations and family dilemmas. They are self-sufficient egotists who would never think of asking someone for help because it would hurt their pride.

Wise leadership always seeks advice. "Most of us want to learn, but we hate like fury to be taught." Consider the son of the king who "forsook the counsel which the old men gave him and took counsel with the young men that were brought up with him, that stood before him" (2 Ch 10:8).

He took their advice. They ignored the elders and went their own way in a self-energized tax reform that had the entire nation in revolt.

Quite in contrast was the apostle Paul. Acts 15 tells the story of his going to the Council of Jerusalem. Honesty and humbly he sought the admonitions and cautions of the church leaders. Rather than taking the attitude that it was Paul and the Holy Spirit against the world, he looked to the sage counsel of others.

Be careful that you do not search until you find someone to confirm your own prejudices and desires and then dare to say, "I sought the suggestions of others." Who counsels you is most important. This proverb is echoed in Proverbs 11:14, "Where no wise guidance is, the people fall: but in the multitude of counselors there is safety."

God seemingly does His best work through a band of men rather than the lone wolf. Seldom, if ever, is the one-man show a success. A multitude of counselors is needed to provide:

1. Encouragement. When the going gets rough, there are many hands to help.

2. Objectivity. Several men will see a problem or project from different perspectives.

3. A sounding board. Having to present your plans to a group of men will help you do a better job in thinking through. Sometimes in seeking their counsel you will see the weaknesses and shallowness of your own pet ideas. Ask God to give you some men with listening ears and hearts in order for you to sound out your ideas.

Above all, take everything to God in prayer. Seek His divine guidance and direction. Do you remember how He is entitled in Isaiah 9:6? "and his name shall be called Wonderful, Counselor."

DO IT BOLDLY AND WHOLLY

"The mind of man plans his way, But the Lord directs his steps." PROVERBS 16:9 (NASB)

"It's these decisions that kill me!" This haunting cry is heard from the lips of the swivel-chair executive as well as thousands of men who want the strokes of life called from God's side of the ledger.

The whole of life is this business of choosing. Decision making is your daily duty. Tragically these decisions often become so mechanical that you hardly realize the importance of what you are deciding.

Big Jim Elliott was a young, rugged pioneer of resolution. Several years ago he and his buddies were martyred by the Auca Indians of South America. Jim had a motivating motto by which he lived and finally died on the shores of the Curaray River: "He is no fool who gives what he cannot keep to gain what he cannot lose."

Early in life, Jim settled with God on what was basic. The bent of his life was always and foremost, what is on the heart of God? In the light of his motto, all personal choices left no doubt on whose side Jim belonged!

"I hate to see things done by halves. If it be right, do it boldly and wholly. If it be wrong, leave it undone, completely."

You, too, must plan your way. There is no substitution for thinking and working out a blueprint for daily living. It is neutrality that curses a man in the hour of decision. How long will you limp between two opinions?

Caesar started a war by leading his army across the Rubicon River contrary to governmental orders. It finally ended with his becoming supreme commander for all of Gaul. It was an irrevocable, decisive step in the conquest of geography.

"Cross the Rubicon." Weakened in character is the man who cannot be decisive. The sidelines of life are full of spectators who refuse to choose. Nothing attempted, nothing accomplished. Never forget, The Lord controls your course. He is always at hand to help with vital decisions.

GIVE BOUNCE TO YOUR LIFE

"A merry heart doeth good like a medicine: but a broken spirit drieth the bones." PROVERBS 17:22

How refreshing it is to meet a good-humored Christian, not a giddy guy, not a shallow-witted joker, not the jester of a slapstick variety, but a man filled with wholesome joy and refreshing buoyancy. No one enjoys a sour self-centered pickle face.

A cheerful heart makes for a cheerful personality. Replace your moods of depression and gripes of complaint with what the Great Physician wrote on His scriptural prescription pad: "Be of good cheer."

A merry heart can be yours not intermittently, but continually. It is not dependent upon the condition of your health, nervous system, nor bank account, but dependent solely upon the promises of God. This is not the superficial optimism and mirth of some TV comedian, for that is well described in Ecclesiastes 7:6 as "the crackling of thorns under a pot."

Follow these directions for a merry heart:

1. Stay on good terms with God. Fear and depression are often the result of a feeling of guilt and a result of conviction of sin. Confess and ask forgiveness.

2. Stay on good terms with your fellow man. Keep your conscience void of offense. Never allow resentment, jealousy or envy to build up. Keep short accounts with your wife, your children, your brother and your neighbors.

3. Never grumble. A complaining Christian is a paradox to the world. Be genuinely thankful. Gratitude gives chase to self-pity and discontent. Every annoyance is an opportunity for victory.

4. Practice having a merry heart. Show it. Smile! Develop with God's help a hearty laugh and an enjoyment of the bright things in life. Work on the cheerful voice and a tone to your conversation that is joyful and cheery.

"They looked to Him, and were radiant; their faces shall never blush for shame or be confused" (Ps 34:5, Amplified).

THE SAGA OF THE SLUGGARD

"Slothfulness casteth into a deep sleep; and an idle soul shall suffer hunger." PROVERBS 19:15

Few men have ever lived in Ulcer Gulch due to hard work. Fewer have died from overwork. One honest man remarked, "I love work. I can sit and watch it by the hour." Honest and hard work is exalted in the book of Proverbs. The sluggard is exiled. He is a fool, for he is a dreamer, not a doer!

The bed may be preferred to battle, but medals of honor are never passed out to the slothful on his king-sized mattress. This soft and flabby life is usually the wrong life. Sleep is easier than labor, self-indulgence easier than enduring hardness, doing nothing easier than doing something.

Brains, wealth, and personality are no substitute for hard work. Tilling the soil by the sweat of the brow is fast becoming a lost desire.

Nine other verses in Proverbs tell us the tragic story of the slothful man. Look them up and study them for your heart profit:

12:24—Leadership shall never be his portion.
12:27—Lazily he lives upon the earnings of others.
15:19—Problems and difficulties engulf him constantly.
18:9 —He is trifling and careless in his responsibilities.
19:24—He hugs himself in ease.
21:25—Refusal to produce is his trademark.
22:13—There are continual illusions of dangers to his life.
24:30—There is total breakdown in management of his business and home.
26:14—He is in love with his complacency.

Now is the hour to shake off apathetic inaction! Resist that cozy outlook to life.

"Let us not allow slackness to spoil our work and let us keep the fires of the spirit burning, as we do our work for the Lord" (Ro 12:11, Phillips).

A PASSION FOR PRINCIPLE

"Diverse weights [one for buying and another for selling] and diverse measures, both of them are exceedingly offensive and abhorrent to the Lord." PROVERBS 20:10 (Amplified)

There is critical need for Christianity in the world today. Give us a band of business and professional men who have a passion for principle. Too many of us are like the fellow that Longfellow wrote about: "He doesn't allow his principles to take root, but pulls them up every now and then, as a little boy does the flowers he has planted, to see if they are growing."

We often pull them up, not just to see if they are growing, but so that others cannot see them. This is known in the business world as "winking at the right time." Where are the men of one standard, absolutes, moral and spiritual ethics that rule their personal, business and social lives?

Thirty-five inches just is not a yard. Fifteen ounces will never make a pound. A used automobile with 37,894 miles and its mileage turned back still has traveled 37,894 miles. If I worked for a man just seven and a half hours, what right have I to charge eight hours?

Live on the square. If the United States government has a Bureau of Standards, how much more does the kingdom of heaven keep good accounts of our business dealings. "But thou shalt have a perfect and just weight, a perfect and just measure shalt thou have: that thy days may be lengthened in the land which the Lord thy God giveth thee. For all that do such things, and all that do unrighteously, are an abomination unto the Lord thy God." (Deu 25:15-16).

Need is a code of conduct for American leadership. Business ethics, corporation morality and personal internal principles—all these terms mean nothing unless we see each individual man standing alone before the yardstick of God's Holy Scriptures. Go to the Bible if in doubt as to what course of action to take: "He that walketh righteously, and speaketh uprightly; he that despiseth the gain of oppressions, that shaketh his hands from holding of bribes, that stoppeth his ears from hearing of blood, and shutteth his eyes from seeing evil; He shall dwell on high: his place of defence shall be the munitions of rocks: bread shall be given him; his waters shall be sure" (Is 33:15-16).

THE CONTROLLING HAND

"The king's heart is in the hand of the Lord, as the rivers of water: he turneth it whithersoever he will. PROVERBS 21:1

God turns the heart of leadership like a farmer turns water down an irrigation ditch. World-shaking events do not happen outside the boundaries of God's sovereignty. His hand is daily upon the headgates of the heart. He misses nothing! His eyes are not shut, nor is He ever caught napping. It is impossible to wheel and deal behind the back of the Almighty.

God knows all. The unsearchable and unmanageable hearts of world dictators are not only seen by the eye of the Lord but controlled by His hand. What a comfort to know that "all things are naked and opened unto the eyes of him with whom we have to do" (Heb 4:13).

Benjamin Franklin was not particularly noted for his godliness, but surely he possessed a good-sized chunk of realism. "The longer I live, the more convincing proofs I see of this truth . . . God governs in the affairs of man; and if a sparrow cannot fall to the ground without His notice, is it probable that an empire can rise without His aid?"

King Nebuchadnezzar of Babylon in the year 586 B.C. bowed before the King of kings, Jehovah God. A daring young Jewish lad by the name of Daniel with unswerving religious convictions was used by the Lord to speak to this proud and haughty king. Note in Daniel, chapter 4, three times Nebuchadnezzar is reminded of who is in charge. Verses 17, 25 and 32 say "until thou know that the most High ruleth in the kingdom of men, and giveth it to whomsoever He will."

Circumstances and events in the life of a kingdom, nation, or a group of united states, are as threads in the tapestry of time. The Omnipotent God is the weaver.

Man's heart is in God's hand! Be it that of Nebuchadnezzar, Ahab, Herod, Agrippa, Hitler, or your own heart, all are controlled by the hand of the Creator, the Sustainer and the Saviour of the world. King-sized men have to confess: "To will is mine, but not to execute, this is the sole right of God."

"But our God is in the heavens: he hath done whatsoever he hath pleased" (Ps 115:3). Whatever pleases God is the very best for you and me.

NEVER GAMBLE WITH YOUR NAME

"A good name is rather to be chosen than great riches, and loving favour rather than silver and gold." PROVERBS 22:1

A name stands for personality, power and character. To what extraordinary limits men will go in order to get their names before fellow man. Human nature shrinks from remaining anonymous.

But one paramount quality cannot be purchased with money—a good name. Be careful to keep a name well spoken of. Once you develop a bad name, your reputation is bankrupt. To be poor is no disgrace, to have a questionable name is tragic.

Alexander the Great was visiting his troops when he encountered an unshaven, uncouth and drunken soldier. "What's your name, soldier?" he demanded.

"Alexander," replied the soaker.

"My man," commanded the emperor, "either change your conduct or change your name."

Of all the current assets possessed by nobility or the rank and file, a good name heads the list. Choose a priceless reputation rather than financial gain that has gray or black overtones.

Esau chose riches and thereby forfeited his good name. Job chose a good name and thereby temporarily forfeited his fortune.

Take as an illustration the first century disciples of Christ. Migratory, simple and uncluttered with earthly possessions, but for over two thousand years they have had the good name—Christian!

Take another New Testament illustration, Demas. He was careless with his name among good men and took off for the city of Thessalonica where he could gain material success and earthly security. Today the name Demas is synonymous with deserter.

"A good name once broken may possibly be repaired, but the world will always keep their eyes on the spot where the crack was."

"Dead flies cause the ointment of the perfumer to putrefy [and] send forth a vile odor; so does a little folly [in him who is valued for wisdom]—outweigh wisdom and honor" (Ec 10:1, Amplified).

MORE THAN MERE MIMICKING

"My son, give me thine heart, and let thine eyes observe my ways." PROVERBS 23:26

Pacesetting is a basic principle in life. It is the core of a successful home life; the heart of school instruction; the bull's-eye of business. A pacesetter helps to increase another's capacity and enlarge his output in driving to the finish. A pacesetter should build, not break or run other men into the ground.

Find yourself a pacesetter who is a true embodiment of Christianity. Then follow him with an open heart and observing eyes. One without the other would be mere mimicking.

After the tragic death of her husband, Ruth said to her widowed mother-in-law, "Whither thou goest, I will go; and where thou lodgest, I will lodge: thy people shall be my people, and thy God my God" (Ru 1:16). Two verses later it says, "she was stedfastly minded to go with her." One example is more valuable than twenty precepts written in a book. Naomi was a splendid example of a God-fearing believer, and Ruth could see the reflection.

Gideon was a pacesetter for his three hundred men. A united, obedient and faithful band of soldiers routed the hordes of the Midianites by following a simple law of warfare. "And he said unto them, 'Look on me, and do likewise: and, behold, when I come to the outside of the camp, it shall be that, as I do, so shall ye do'" (Judg 7:17).

The apostle Paul was not an overestimated egotist when he said: "Be ye followers of me, even as I also am of Christ" (1 Co 11:1). This is family talk. Paul the pacesetter was down the experience road a little farther than his children in the Lord. It was not a vertical relationship of lordship but a horizontal link of companions. Be careful not to get your eyes on men rather than Jesus Christ. It should be obvious that the pacesetter is following the Lord.

"After all, you may have ten thousand teachers in the Christian faith, but you cannot have many fathers! . . . that is why I implore you to follow the footsteps of me your father" (1 Co 4:15-16, Phillips).

ALWAYS TOO SOON TO QUIT

"If thou faint in the day of adversity, thy strength is small."
                                    PROVERBS 24:10

The fainthearted droop and wilt while the stronghearted fight. The size of a man is clearly seen when the chips are down and he is under pressure. In these days of uncertainty and crisis, there is one thing for sure—there will be days of adversity, adverse finances or health; reverses in business or family affairs; dark days of death and discouragement.

How do you react to adversity? If your strength is small, your spirit will sink, your knees cave in, and you will come completely unglued. It would be a sign that you are not a man of any resolution, without any firmness of thought, of any consideration, of any faith, if you cannot bear up under a negative change in your conditions.

Job had his day of adversity. The roof caved in, the bottom dropped out, the walls collapsed, and the top blew off. Joseph had his prison, Daniel his lion's den, and Paul his shipwrecks.

Did these men call it quits and faint in the day of adversity? Here is how they might tell us about their hour of trial:

Joseph: "Muscles are built in use and opposition. God has given me the opportunity to prove my trust in Him."

Daniel: "It is one thing to be vice-president in the sunshine; quite another to be a Christian in the darkness of the pit."

Paul: "I am ready for anything and equal to anything through Him who infuses inner strength into me."

Faint not! Flee not! Fail not! It is always too soon to quit.

"If thou hast run with the footmen, and they have wearied thee, then how canst thou contend with horses? and if in the land of peace, wherein thou trustedst, they wearied thee, then how wilt thou do in the swelling of Jordan?" (Jer 12:5).

AN ACHING TOOTH

"Confidence in an unfaithful man in time of trouble is like a broken tooth, and a foot out of joint." PROVERBS 25:19

Have you ever wondered why an apparently ordinary fellow, with very mediocre training and average personality, is found to be on the top of the success pile?

The answer often lies in his dependability.

He is the man you can count on when the chips are down. He delivers the goods no matter how rough the road. He keeps his word and makes good on his promises.

The faithful man is indeed a rare individual.

In the time of trouble confidence in men is most needed. It hurts when the sentry sleeps in the field of battle.

It hurts when businessmen are "careless promisers."

It hurts like fury when formerly trusted friends are not reliable in counsel nor trustworthy in advice.

An unfaithful man hurts like a bad tooth or an ailing leg which affect the entire physical and emotional system of man.

Your mouth and your foot represent your talk and your walk. Both are seriously influenced by broken confidence.

How must Jesus Christ have suffered before the Golgotha agony when His disciples proved amazingly disloyal! His own men "put His foot out of joint" long before the soldiers of Caesar came to break His legs (Jn 19:32).

Think of the ache experienced by the apostle Paul when John Mark left him on that first missionary team. Imagine the anguish of John 6:66—"From that time many of His disciples went back, and walked no more with Him."

Answer the call for faithful men.

"Help, Lord; for the godly man ceaseth; for the faithful fail from among the children of men" (Ps 12:1).

MEDDLING OR MENDING?

"He that passeth by, and meddleth with strife belonging not to him, is like one that taketh a dog by the ears." PROVERBS 26:17

If you want to get bitten, stick your nose into someone else's business. Many a man is nursing a sore caused by getting involved in a deal that was absolutely none of his affair. Grab a dog by the ears, and you have really got a howling mess in your hand. It takes all your attention and the biggest question of all is how do you let go without getting bitten?

Meddling is a sure way to lay yourself open to trouble. Meddling is the igniting fire thrown into a barrel of gasoline. This contention is well expressed in Proverbs 30:33: "Surely the churning of milk bringeth forth butter, and the wringing of the nose bringeth forth blood: so the forcing of wrath bringeth forth strife."

There is a time to be the third-person arbitrator, and there is a time to keep right on walking past trouble. The good Samaritan was passing by and quickly got involved in a problem not his own. This was right. This is biblical involvement. This distinction of what is my business when a man is in need, and that which I am to avoid like the plague, was missing in the early days of Moses.

One day in ancient times an Egyptian and a Jew were arguing. The discussion became heated and tempers were on edge. Passing by was Moses. He overheard the battle of words and could not resist the desire to square away this Egyptian. As you read the story in the opening chapters of the book of Exodus, you will quickly realize that Moses grabbed a dog by the ears, and it took forty years for the wound to heal. All because this young leader needed to learn God's lesson: "as much as lieth in you, live peaceably with all men" (Ro 12:18). Moses had a spirit of division, not unity.

Twice the apostle Peter got involved in business not his own. Once it was to his disgrace because he was meddling. That was when he cut off the ear of the high priest's servant.

Another time he got involved in business that was not his own. He and John healed a beggar. But this was not the meddling of strife. This was the ministry of sympathy.

CHAINED LIONS—BOLD CHRISTIANS

"The wicked flee when no man pursueth: but the righteous are bold as a lion." PROVERBS 28:1

Sin guilt makes a man a coward. His own shadow causes fear. He starts to run with no one in pursuit. But not so the righteous man. A clean and clear conscience prevents the plague of the guilt complex.

A man with a clear conscience is bold as a lion! "Not the brute force of a vulgar warrior but the firm resolve of a God-sent soldier."

Learn from Gideon. He hid from God. He was so afraid of himself that he asked for proof positive. But he became so sure of God that he was content with three hundred men, lamps, pitchers and a few blasting trumpets.

He was afraid of himself, but sure of God.

Beware of the paralysis of false humility or ability. Timidity is not manly nor is it godly. It is fear that has stagnated the progress of many Christians.

Remember John Bunyan's Pilgrim on the road to the Celestial City? In dismay one day he cries: "There are lions in the way." And he was right. There were the lions boldly blocking his way. But the lions were chained. As soon as Christian saw this, he boldly moved on.

1. Learn how to come boldly to the throne of grace in prayer. Draw near His throne and receive from the Lord your help, your strength and your power. "Let us therefore approach the throne of grace with fullest confidence, that we may receive mercy for our failures and grace to help in the hour of need" (Heb 4:16, Phillips).

2. Learn how to be bold in sharing Christ with other men, not rude, nor crude, but bold. Be on the offense but not offensive! Peter, in the danger-hour of Calvary, was a moral coward. Later he learned his lesson in the school of Christ and we read: "When they saw the complete assurance of Peter and John, who were obviously uneducated and untrained men, they were staggered" (Ac 4:13, Phillips).

Be bold for Christ's sake. This holy boldness comes from holy living, which only a Holy God can produce,

OBSTINATE AS A MULE

"He, that being often reproved hardeneth his neck, shall suddenly be destroyed, and that without remedy."

PROVERBS 29:1

Is it possible to tease, test and stretch mercy to the point of no return? Parents, pastor, teacher and friends continue to counsel, but the stubborn, self-willed man gets himself against them and God.

Then the roof of circumstances caves in.

Even God has a point beyond which he will not go with an obstinate person. "My spirit shall not always strive with man" (Gen 6:3).

Then there are no more chances to reconsider, no more opportunities to reopen the case, no privilege for repentance. "Without remedy" is written across the life of the man with a hardened neck.

As obstinate as a mule, this man follows the pattern set down for us in the book of Proverbs:

10:17—"He that refuseth reproof erreth."

5:12—His "heart despised reproof."

12:1 —"He that hateth reproof is brutish."

Refuse, despise, hate is the downward course of this fixed and unyielding heart. Is it any wonder that there comes a time when there is no possible remedy? "For if God wounds, who can heal?"

Esau sold out to the flesh. "Afterward, when he wanted to inherit the blessing, he was rejected, for he found no place for recalling the decision, although with tears he sought for the blessing" (Heb 12:17, Berkeley).

Repentance is not sorrow for sin which we keep on committing; nor is repentance sorrow for the consequences of sin; neither is it changing outward conduct and attitudes while still loving the sin.

Repentance is to think it over again, to rethink life.

We need this rethinking about God. We need to think again about ourselves and our relationship with Him and with our fellow man. How many chances does a man get?

"He that covereth his sins shall not prosper: but whoso confesseth and forsaketh them shall have mercy" (Pr 28:13).

GREATNESS IN MINIATURE

"There be four things which are little upon the earth, but they are exceeding wise." PROVERBS 30:24

There is always the danger of admiring bodily bulk. Daily we are tempted to judge by external beauty or to be overly impressed with muscular strength. Greatness is often in miniature. The weak, the little, the insignificant can teach us lessons we could not learn from the tiger or the elephant.

Littleness does not mean nothingness. Solomon wisely illustrates this truth in Proverbs 30:25-28 and uses four puny insects as examples.

The ants are not strong (v. 25) yet they have a built-in sense of doing the right thing at the right time. They work in the summer so that when they cannot work in the winter they have all they need. From the ants we learn prudence.

The conies are not mighty (v. 26). These tiny rabbits or field mice have an uncanny understanding of their environment. Because of this realization of their weakness and lack of strength, they live in the rocks. Wide awake is the man that has a true estimation of his assets and liabilities. The wise man flees to the Rock, a refuge, and hiding place that David sings about in Psalm 18:2. From the cony brood learn the lesson of perception.

The locusts are not organized (v. 27), yet they go forth to divide the spoil and not one of them is appointed the chief. They keep together, pull together, and in one accord get the job done. Throughout the world they are known as pesky little creatures that move across the face of the earth like a might army all fused and combined as one. A challenge for men of all races, colors or creeds —if we be one in Christ, we are all part of the same unified body. From the locust band learn the lesson of partnership.

Spiders are not wanted (v. 28). Despite their insignificance they end up in the king's palace. Everyone is against them, sweeping away their webs and daily attempting to destroy them. Yet even when all their work is destroyed, they immediately start all over again. They are like Joseph, an unknown country boy in the Pharaoh's palace who ended up on top despite every attempt to keep him down. From the spider learn the lesson of persistence.

THE GODLY HOMEMAKER

"Favour is deceitful, and beauty is vain: but a woman that feareth the Lord, she shall be praised." PROVERBS 31:30

The grand finale of the book of Proverbs is a praise of the godly homemaker, a portrait not of the ideal woman or wife, but "mother in the home."

When a man goes to choose a woman, there is a good checklist to begin with in Proverbs 31:10-31.

William R. Wallace paid his immortal tribute to motherhood in these familiar words: "The hand that rocks the cradle is the hand that rules the world." Think of the mothers of Augustine, of the Wesley brothers, of D. L. Moody or of Billy Graham.

When you see an unusual son, nine times out of ten you will discover an unusual mother. George Washington had a pious and devoted mother; the mother of Nero was a murderess. Sir Walter Scott had parents who were lovers of poetry, music and the arts. The mother of the intemperate Lord Byron was a proud and violent woman. For good or bad, like mother like child!

Consider the godly woman, Hannah (1 Sa 1:2). She was a great woman and bore a great son given to her by God in answer to her prayer. It is no small wonder that Samuel wrought a great deliverance in Israel as a leader among men.

Hannah knew her God. She also knew His promises. Most of all, Hannah knew her place as a mother in the home. She sought not a career, a prominent ministry, not some spectacular position in the community. Her life was wrapped up in her God and her home responsibilities. God is still looking for twentieth century Hannahs!

THE CARBORUNDUM OF COMRADES

"Iron sharpeneth iron; so a man sharpeneth the countenance of his friend." PROVERBS 27:17

Do you feel bored, dull, and inactive? This verse tells us that in order to look sharp, feel sharp, and be sharp, you should have a close friend.

It is tragic to find lonely men who have no one close to them, No one with whom to share their heart, no one with whom they can pray about the intimate things of their soul.

Iron can be sharpened with a file. The cutting edge of a steel knife needs to be whet on the carborundum. Cutlery always needs the hone! In the same way, a man has a built-in need for a friend who does not just cut and slice but sharpens and quickens.

"Two are better than one. . . . For if they fall, the one will lift up his companion; but woe to the one alone who falls, when there is no other to lift him up" (Ec 4:9-10, Berkeley).

Caleb and Joshua stood together in the minority report committee when they returned from scouting the Promised Land. Abraham was the friend of God. Not so much by what he did, but by what he was. God sharpened the rough old Jew into a polished diamond for His glory.

Have you ever heard of Zabud? King Solomon called him "the king's friend" in 1 Kings 4:5.

Do not try to stand alone. Spend time with a comrade in Christ who will help sharpen your wits, share in your conversation, and shape your future.

"When two good men get together, it brightens their looks, cheers their spirits, puts a briskness and liveliness into their countenance, and gives them an air that other men are pleased with. This is the filing that makes men smooth and bright and fit for buisness."

Good men are made sharp by those that are good but bad men's lust and passions can also dull one of God's sharpest instruments.

What does it take to have an iron friend? Be one!

Your choicest friendship will be like phosphorus—best seen when all is dark.

SWALLOW THAT GOSSIP

"He that answereth a matter before he heareth it, it is folly and shame unto him." PROVERBS 18:13

Is passing judgment upon others ever the duty of a Christian?

Never, if it is prejudgment. If you come up with a verdict before hearing the facts of a case, you are prejudiced. Folly and shame are your rewards. This has to do with gossip. Hold that juicy news you know about. Swallow it. In many cases, silence is golden. "In the multitude of words there wanteth not sin: but he that refraineth his lips is wise" (Pr 10:19).

This has to do with counseling. Don't start talking until you have heard a person out. Give him an opportunity to share, then answer! Jumping to conclusions is poor sport in conversation. It usually terminates the talk! Hasty chatter is foolish and humiliating. A ready wit is for play and fun, but do business with solid judgment and wisdom. Do not pass judgment until you are fully informed.

This has to do with criticizing. A harsh, intolerant fleshly mind is in no position to act as critic. Such a person cuts others down to raise himself up.

"After all, who are you to criticize the servant of somebody else, especially when that somebody else is God?" (Ro 14:4, Phillips).

Study the book of Proverbs and what it has to say about the tongue. Scores of verses indicate that a man's unguarded talk betrays the real man!

Hasty conclusions and a biased spirit reveal a warped, twisted and superficial heart. "Out of the abundance of the heart the mouth speaketh" (Mt 12:34).

"There is nothing which most men pay less attention to than their words. They go through a day, speaking and talking without thought or reflection, and seem to fancy that if they do what is right, it matters little what they say." Give yourself the little three-way test before speaking about someone: Is it kind? Is it necessary? Is it true?

"Set a watch, O Lord, before my mouth; keep the door of my lips" (Ps 141:3).

NOTHING TO DO BUT TO BE

"Blessed is the man that heareth me, watching daily at my gates, waiting at the posts of my doors." PROVERBS 8:34

The hurried and churning man knows nothing of this promise. The price tag is too high—hearing, watching, and waiting. Get apart in solitude so that you can hear God's voice, watch His movements, and wait for His bidding. Nothing to do but to be! Blessed is the man who takes time out for inaction with nothing to do but think.

Phil Wylie had a fascinating article, "Just Thinking," in *Ladies Home Journal*. He says, "Today, a daydreaming boy is prodded to meaningless activity by nervous parents who fear that solitude is somehow dangerous. A boy in reverie is hurriedly sent down the street to play games, lest he becomes anti-social.

"As a result, young people pass through adolescence with no practice in testing their inner selves. They grow up mindless, in effect, because they are not encouraged to explore their minds.

"We believe what we hear—not what we think. Our minds have shrunk from disuse, and from the avoidance of situations which demand serious reflection.

"If we Americans do not start to think, if we let slip the old practice of self-exile in a silent place, we shall presently become a nation of superficial men and women, identical and interchangeable. Nobody will be able to find anything special in anybody else. Our opinion, like our possessions, will be prefabricated. Leadership will become exaggerated examples of the mediocrity of the masses."

It is not enough just to meditate. Happy is the man who hears God. Make sure your meditation centers in Christ and the affairs of His kingdom. "Be still and let God speak."

"Most religious men are so busy with spreading or defending Christianity that they have little time and less inclination for quiet meditation and communion with God. Men need deep inner resolution and planning to get a clear space to be quiet and look at God."

Part 4

A CHALLENGE FROM ECCLESIASTES

when the ceiling is zero

The book of Ecclesiastes has been viewed as a writing of disillusionment. But it can be a rich source of counsel for days of trouble and depression, offering solid, practical help to correct and encourage; and it is full of suggestions on how to weather the storms of life that assail personal faith.

Solomon, who wrote Ecclesiastes through the inspiration of the Holy Spirit, had problems and doubts, but he also had an anchor for his soul.

Are you trying to live by the ethics of expediency? Are you bewildered by the seeming inequalities of life? Do you find yourself wandering about in the wilderness of spiritual desolation? Then accept these challenges from Ecclesiastes.

A VOYAGER AFTER TRUTH

"Vapor of vapors and futility of futilities, says the Preacher, vapor of vapors and futility of futilities, all is vanity—emptiness, falsity and vainglory." ECCLESIASTES 1:2 (Amplified)

Work, eat, and sleep then draw your pay so you can work, eat and sleep then draw your pay so you can do it all over again. This is squirrel-cage living in the twentieth century.

Men wear out their life-machinery in the race for false happiness. There is immense activity but no satisfaction of attainment. Solomon writes this book of Ecclesiastes to show us the vanity of the world and its inability to give happiness.

Ecclesiastes is to be read, and reread, and remembered. Many men write off the futility of this world but know nothing of it, not so King Solomon. He had tasted the depths of it all. His head was full of its wisdom and his belly full of its "cheating treasures." He would groan with Job: "I am tired of it; I would not live always. Leave me alone" (Job 7:16, Berkeley).

Ecclesiastes is the logbook of a voyager after truth. The twelve chapters tell of storms, rocky shoals, sand bars and a rugged trip till he safely reaches the desired haven. "Fear God, and keep his commandments: for this is the whole duty of man" (Ec 12:13).

It has been suggested The Song of Solomon was penned in fiery youth; Proverbs is a production of Solomon's prime manhood; Ecclesiastes the earnest seeking of latter years as he was longing for clues for unsolved difficulties. This book is the struggle of inquiring man seeking reality.

Solomon knew the purposelessness of things, the emptiness of learning, honor, sensual delights, power, riches and great possessions without God. Solomon carries two threads throughout the book. One is based upon personal experience. This is called the "I" section. This series of terse and pointed sayings strike fire in the heart of any honest thinking man. The other thread is the "Thou" section of this shrewd philosophy. In these verses, Solomon reflects upon experiences that all men down through the ages will encounter.

This brilliant king is telling us: "If you fall, hasten to recover and get back on your feet; then take a good healthy look at where you have been." Solomon is also telling us: "Don't let the uniformity of life flatten your interest in the great miracle of every fresh day."

Drive a shaft clear down through all the superficial strata, and lay the first fundamental stones of your life upon the Rock of Ages.

CLINGING TO SOAP BUBBLES

"What is wrong cannot be righted; it is water over the dam; and there is no use thinking of what might have been."
ECCLESIASTES 1:15 (Living Bible)

"What a mess I have made of things."

So confessed a youthful singing star and Hollywood actor. His confession continues: "Success came too early, too fast and there was too much. Life was too good, too exciting, too luxurious. I just couldn't believe it would last. Hence, somewhere along the line in my fierce clawing to reach top, I must have lost my sense of values."

This young man's life had become messed-up, insipid and filled with disillusionment because of the way he invested his life. His value rating was zero. With mixed emotions and hazy values he concluded the article: "Fears brought wild panic. I wrestled at night. I jumped like a pogo stick during the day. I took pills to go to sleep and I took pills to stay awake. What a mess!"

This is the honest appraisal of a worldling's success. He had latched on to perishables and found himself clinging to soap bubbles. His greed for gold and clamor for glamour left him empty and alone. As with Solomon, the years of his life had been propped up and finally they gave out under the weight of time and true values.

Can these wrong values ever be righted? Now that the water is over the dam, what comes next?

The gold standard is man's evaluation of worth. God's standard of true treasure is based upon motive of possession, durability and Christ-centeredness. If you are clawing to reach the top, you have already missed God's estimation of wealth.

Jesus talked in the Sermon on the Mount about man's evaluation of true worth and assets. The men of His day were concerned for clothing, food and earthly security. Their appraisal of life was much like that of the Hollywood actor. It was at this point that Jesus said: "Lay not up for yourselves treasures upon earth, where moth and rust corrupt, and where thieves break through and steal" (Mt 6:19).

The sweeping assertion that "things cannot be changed," that "what is going to be is going to be" is not true! Things can change. Your estimation of values can change. You can change. The past is past, but the future does not need to be a mess.

"When someone becomes a Christian he becomes a brand new person inside. He is not the same any more. A new life has begun!" (2 Co 5:17, Living Bible).

BANKRUPT IN SUCCESS

"I made me great works . . . I gathered me also silver and gold . . . so I was great, and increased more than all."
ECCLESIASTES 2:4, 8-9

Here is the autobiography of a leader who was bankrupt in his success, the vivid picture of the frustration of greatness. He has everything and yet his accountant concludes the annual report with these words: "Possessing all things, yet having nothing." (Compare 2 Co 6:10.)

Solomon had experimented down three pathways for happiness—earthly wisdom, giddy mirth and sensual pleasures. All was empty and hollow.

"I will make me great works." Perhaps in the building of an empire there will be an end to all this restlessness. Is there gratification through performance? So Solomon built an empire.

The action verbs of these sentences show his drive and dedicated resolve. "I made . . . I built . . . I planted . . . I got . . . I gathered."

Solomon built great structures and housing projects. He took agriculture seriously with gardens, vineyards and orchards. Reforestation was high on his priority list. No financial holds were barred as he poured in money for canals, waterworks and reservoirs.

Growth means jobs and jobs mean people. With the population explosion, Solomon had to increase food production through "large possessions of cattle, herds and flocks."

He loved his work. His business was a challenge. There surely was no disappointment in the profit column.

Yet, when this man reviewed his great works with all the cost, care and toil, there was not the heart ease and satisfaction he wanted (v. 11).

In the pursuit for happiness, he comes to another dead end. Again he learns, "A man's life consisteth not in the abundance of the things which he possesseth" (Lk 12:15).

Solomon built a nation for God but failed in building his personal life in God. Success in doing but failure in being. This wisest of all men who spent his life majoring on the minors should have listened to his father who said, "One thing have I desired of the Lord, that will I seek after . . . to behold the beauty of the Lord, and to enquire in His temple" (Ps 27:4).

THE WHEELS OF PROVIDENCE

"To every thing there is a season, and a time to every purpose under the heaven." ECCLESIASTES 3:1

Why do things happen that bring so much sorrow and heartache? Is it true that our disappointments are God's appointments?

Be assured, nothing just happens to God's man. There are no mere accidents in your life. In this world of perpetual change, fluctuating events, and shifting circumstances, it is great to have a stable center that says, "My times are in thy hand" (Ps 31:15).

Listen to the way that John Wilder puts it: "A loving Father has obligated Himself and guaranteed that everything that takes place in the lives of those who love Him is for good.

"That means that every tear, every sorrow, every misfortune, every catastrophe, every calamity, even hurricanes and tornadoes, famines and freezes, depressions and plagues, sickness, pain, disappointments, and even death—all things—work together, cooperate, move in a mighty teamwork for good to them that love God."

Here in Ecclesiastes 3:2-8 there are fourteen maxims that cover the rampart of events that come into our lives. Read the list! Everything is covered, industrial relations to human labor, social and business transactions, human feelings and public service, plus life and death, fun and sorrow, and ending with international war and peace.

What are lessons for our hearts from this page in Solomon's logbook? First of all, there is no fatalism here. Man's confidence must be based upon a practical dependence in God. The God who is neither fickle nor shortsighted is intensely interested in you!

Finally, look at the Creator, not the creature. He makes no mistakes. Nothing happens behind His back. Throughout the whole there is the perfection of His harmony.

"Moreover we know that to those who love God, who are called according to his plan, everything that happens fits into a pattern for good" (Ro 8:28, Phillips).

A MAN OF VISION

"He hath made every thing beautiful in his time: also he hath set the world in their heart, so that no man can find out the work that God maketh from the beginning to the end."
ECCLESIASTES 3:11

So often in living we lack vision. Our horizons have no vastness. We are like men in the bottom of a well. In looking up all we see is a little patch of the blue sky.

Microscopic is our vision when we need to be telescopic.

"He hath set the world in their heart." From the Gobi Desert to Guatemala, from Massachusetts to Montezuma this panorama is what is on God's heart and He wants to get it into our hearts. Vision is standing where God stands and from His vantage point seeing what He sees.

Vision is not only perspective, but it gives focus. The eyes of a man of vision see not only the Oriental temple, but the masses of people blindly worshipping there. His eyes are not just the eyes of a spectator that enjoys the ball game, but fails to see the crowd.

In God's administration of world affairs, He has not left His men without the faculty of appreciating the deep-seated sense of eternity in purposes and destinies.

If you look at your circumstances through His eyes, you do not see the size of a Goliath. It is thrilling to know how big the Lord really is. A slingshot and smooth stones take on atomic proportions when viewed within His plan and purposes.

If you catch glimpses of God's high and holy purposes, then it is easier to trust Him for what you cannot see and understand.

The story is told of Napoleon's soldiers carrying a map of the world over their hearts. Why? So they would not be thinking of the mud, shortage of food and tired bodies. Daily this military leader wanted his men to think in terms of world conquest.

Think big. Think of the world. Get in step with your Creator who alone can give a true view of eternity and the big picture.

This verse tells me that there are many things that Almighty God is doing that I cannot comprehend, but I can trust Him that the timing is beautiful and what He wants me to know I can know for "eternity has been placed in my heart!"

God, keep me from shortsightedness. Give to me eyes that see with a conquerable optimism in contrast to a defeated pessimism. Lord, enable me to do some spiritual soaring both in sight and service.

The man of vision is always the man of venture.

THE SECRET OF WITHDRAWAL

"Better is an handful with quietness, than both the hands full with travail and vexation of spirit." ECCLESIASTES 4:6

Life seems to be full of the futility of earthly endeavor. It is daily a cycle from crisis, to calm, to complacency, and then back to crisis again.

One western banker compares our nation to a small boy walking on a fence. After awhile he got so good at it that he quit worrying about falling off. Just when he is cocksure about his balance, flop! Normalcy gives way to a new sense of urgency.

Dean Somers of Buffalo School of Administration writes about our business community living in "an atmosphere of controlled panic." To get our vanguard out of the rear guard we must go in for a crash program that produces "economical jitters in the light of rolling readjustments."

Living on the side of a volcano, life for you may seem like a small, sunny Pacific island with warm breezes, swaying palm trees and luxurious living. But one day the sky will darken, the earth shake and the fire and lava of crisis will belch out of the extinct volcano. Chaos reigns instead of calm. Such a world so full of excitement and despair is empty of peace and quietness.

The mind of man is restless until it rests in Jehovah God. Human love yearns and lusts, "seeking something to fasten upon until it touches God and clings in peace to Him."

Full of business and activity? How about a handful of quietness? Is this a dimension to your life?

So many people need a handful of quietness in the midst of the marketplace and work-a-day world. You must experience peace to know it. You need to practice quietness to feel it and enjoy it. A calm spirit and stillness of soul is like a lotion on a bee sting. It takes away the irritation although the puncture remains.

In an hour of inner emptiness and purposelessness, have you learned the secret of disengaging yourself from the hustle and bustle in order to quietly meditate and reflect?

A handful of quietness is found by getting up a little early in the morning for some good old-fashioned "quiet time" with God. In a place of withdrawal, bring a quiet heart and wait upon our Saviour to make Himself known in the holy hush of prayer.

"But as for me, my contentment is not in wealth but in seeing you and knowing all is well between us. And when I awake in heaven, I will be fully satisfied, for I will see you face to face" (Ps 17:15, Living Bible).

DON'T BE A LONER

"Two are better than one; because they have a good reward for their labour." ECCLESIASTES 4:9

A red hot coal left *alone* soon loses its vital glow!

This need for togetherness is seen in the European Common Market, mutual funds, farmer's cooperatives, the Brotherhood of Trainmen and the Fellowship of Christian Athletes.

Men have learned to associate rather than stand alone. United hearts and energies do a terrific job in contrast with isolation. Be it in business, industry, government, classroom or upon the battlefield, there is misery in solitude.

Back in the beginning of things, God took a good look at Adam and came up with this evaluation: "It is not good that the man should be alone."

Here in the fourth chapter of Ecclesiastes, we have three illustrations where two are better than one: *if* they fall, *if* they are in bed together, *if* they are waging a war. Read verses 10-12 for your personal profit. Solomon is reminding us that this togetherness will sweeten our physical labor, soothe the sting of our troubles and give zest to daily living.

Two for one. Is this the reason that Jesus Christ sent out His disciples two by two? The book of Acts is the story of penetration of the Roman empire by God's men, as they traveled two by two (Ac 13:2; 15:35-40)

God's instruments of action are almost always in pairs. Consider the human body: hands, feet, eyes, ears and legs. God's men of action are those who have learned well the lesson of teamwork and unity.

"Two are better than one." Enjoy the communion of the saints. We are members of "the same body." Accept the challenge from Proverbs 27:9: "Ointment and perfume rejoice the heart: so doth the sweetness of a man's friend by hearty counsel."

"Two are better than one." Do not try to carry on all by yourself. You are not big enough, strong enough or wise enough to go it alone. The apostle Paul had several heart-binding friends. Here is what he says about one named Epaphroditus: "He has been to me brother, fellow worker, comrade-in-arms, as well as being the messenger" (Phil 2:25, Phillips).

"Two are better than one." Do not try to go on any longer without the Lord. He is the "friend that sticketh closer than a brother."

"A friend loveth at all times, and a brother is born for adversity" (Pr 17:17).

WE HATE TO BE TAUGHT

"Better is a poor and a wise child than an old and foolish king, who will no more be admonished." ECCLESIASTES 4:13

Every man who aspires to top performance must be willing to accept suggestions for constructive change. From the cradle to the grave, an open heart to gentle reproof is in absolute.

Mature leadership that rejects admonition is to be pitied. All the years of experience, all organizational skills, all sharp managerial acumen, all these are cancelled out by bullheaded refusal of sage and wise counsel.

"Except ye become as little children" who are teachable, malleable and humble in heart. Children are not usually bound by tradition, impressed by their own importance, nor victims of ceremony, ritual and calloused independence.

The foolish king has lowered the throne beneath the high chair. The very quality that got him to the top as departed. Well can it be said of him: "He gives admonition by the bucketful but accepts it by the grain!"

King Rehoboam is a good illustration (1 Ki 12:1-8). He had the hearts of his people but lost it all by the rejection of admonition. He split the kingdom through the refusal to take wise warning.

Winston Churchill must have had this foolish leader in mind when he said: "We all want to learn, but we all hate to be taught."

The measure of you as a leader might be defined as you answer some of these following questions:

Do you respond positively to criticism and reprimands?

Do you seek out the counsel of others and then with an open heart attempt to make the necessary changes?

Do you harbor resentments toward those who are seeking to help you?

Do you feel that your heart is basically proud, aloof and independent?

An admonition is likened unto a red light. It is a warning of danger ahead. It is a caution to proceed ever so carefully. It is counsel that a wise leader will follow fully.

"Able also to admonish one another" (Ro 15:14).

LEARN THROUGH LISTENING

"Never enter God's house carelessly; draw near him to listen, and then your service is better than what fools offer—for all a fool knows is how to do wrong."
ECCLESIASTES 5:1 (Moffatt)

A man hears what he is listening for!

The acoustical equipment located on either side of your head has a special purpose. Hanging of pencils, hooking your glasses or holding up an oversized hat—these uses are the obvious.

"Bow down thine ear, and hear the words of the wise, and apply thine heart unto my knowledge" (Pr 22:17). Learn through listening. On the average, most of us listen forty per cent of the day to something—good or bad.

Do not switch off your mind. Listening is hard work. It demands that you give eye contact, distraction discipline and emotional focus. "There is no such thing as an uninteresting subject; there are only uninterested people."

Let me suggest a three-point plan for lending your ear.

First, check on where you hear the Word of God spoken. It is great to have your own personal intake of Scripture, but you need to systematically find out what others have to say. This opens up fresh avenues for thought and evaluation. Associate closely with a Bible-preaching pastor and teacher. Make sure you are open for every available opportunity to hear sound teaching from men of God.

Second, how do you hear? Sit where you will not be disturbed. When you first get to your place in church or a meeting, have a word of prayer asking that God will meet the need of your heart. As you listen, have an attitude of reverence, appreciation, imagination, expectancy and most of all, "Act on the Word, instead of merely listening to it and deluding yourselves" (Ja 1:22, Moffatt). Carry your Bible, paper and pencil; these tools help mightily in the battle for concentration.

Last of all, have an ear of discernment as to what you are hearing. Do not swallow everything. You can hear with your ears and still not understand nor discern. Salvation, conviction, praise and guidance are the results for any man who has ears to hear and wants to receive.

He who listens first, serves God best later. Only the fool refuses the voice of God. The difference between doing right or wrong is often tied in with the listening ear.

"The full soul loatheth an honeycomb; but to the hungry soul every bitter thing is sweet" (Pr 27:7).

PAY WHAT YOU VOW

"When you vow a vow or make a pledge to God, do not put off paying it; for God has no pleasure in fools [those who witlessly mock Him]. Pay what you vow!"
ECCLESIASTES 5:4 (Amplified)

Circumstances cannot stop you, lack of money cannot stop you, wicked men and their plots cannot stop you, but you can. Pay what you vow!

Nothing hardens a man's heart, stiffens his will and sears his conscience as to be brought to the point of being "red hot" in a promise of good resolution and spiritual conviction and then to cool down to being a careless promiser.

Jonah was commissioned to go. He was bound by a sacred and constraining obligation to head east for Nineveh. His light commitment was put to the challenge. Jonah sadly shook his head sideways and fled from the presence of the Lord. He said "I will" with his mouth but "I won't" with his heart.

Agreements are sacred. Promises are to be kept. Your word must be as good as your name on the dotted line. Contracts are considered by some as mere scraps of paper, but this must not be so with a man of God.

The psalmist praised God for His faithfulness regarding His promises. "He hath remembered his covenant for ever, the word which he commanded to a thousand generations" (Ps 105:8).

Do you think that God, who believes in keeping a vow at any cost, will deal lightly with a man who will not keep up his end of the deal? Have you made a resolution in days gone by that you have put off and put off? Months have run into years and that pledge to God still needs to be fulfilled.

Promises made in times of difficulty are too often forgotten when fairer days come along. The psalmist reminds us that those vows are still waiting to be fulfilled. "I will pay thee my vows, which my lips have uttered, and my mouth hath spoken, when I was in trouble" (Ps 66:13-14).

Jonah learned the hard way. His refusal to keep his vow caused him to slip down, down and still farther down. At the very bottom, he met God. In a prayer of conviction and confession, Jonah prayed: "But I will sacrifice unto thee with the voice of thanksgiving; I will pay that that I have vowed. Salvation is of the Lord" (Jon 2:9).

THE WORSHIP OF IDOLS

"He that loveth silver shall not be satisfied with silver; nor he that loveth abundance with increase: this is also vanity. When goods increase, they are increased that eat them: and what good is there to the owners thereof, saving the beholding of them with their eyes?" ECCLESIASTES 5:10-11

Excessive love for anything makes a sham of God's first commandment. "Thou shalt have no other gods before me." Any object which produces passionate devotion is an imposter. God allows no rivals.

"They actually made a calf in those days, . . . and grew festive over what their own hands had manufactured" (Ac 7:41, Moffatt). To make something and then bow before it is idolatry. To love success, ambition, prominence and possessions is to retain an idol on the throne of your heart.

It is man's nature to worship. If he does not worship the one and only true God, then the heart will invent its god or gods!

Idolatry is not limited to the pagans of the darkest jungle or the worshipers of a Buddha. Whenever a man longs for what he dares not do, hungers after what he must not have, lusts for what he has no business loving, this is the start of idolatry.

"Man cannot live by bread alone, nor by plastics, nor electronics nor miracle metals. This generation needs more than the things that man's hands can produce. When gadgets become our gods, watch out!"

Watch out for three tempting and fascinating idols. First there is *gold*. What a powerful, attractive and yet dissatisfying idol. No wonder Jesus Christ said to His men, You cannot worship both God and money.

The second idol is that of *goods,* that which I have and control, not only my own, but that which belongs to others. To lust after the goods of another is as serious as idolatry.

The third idol you may worship is a *good time*. Eat, drink and be merry. Is it any wonder that Paul warns youthful Timothy concerning men who are; "Lovers of pleasure more than lovers of God" (2 Ti 3:4, Berkeley).

"The lesson we must learn, my brothers, is that at all costs to avoid worshiping a false god. I am speaking unto you as intelligent men: think over what I am saying" (1 Co 10:14, Phillips).

THE GODDESS CALLED MONEY

"God has given to some men very great wealth and honor, so that they can have everything they want . . . Though a man lives a thousand years twice over, but doesn't find contentment—well, what's the use?" ECCLESIASTES 6:2, 6 (Living Bible).

Money has caused almost as much trouble as the devil himself. Men ruin their health for it, wreck their homes, forfeit their integrity, and sacrifice their lives.

Some men worship money. Some beg, some borrow, some steal it. A few inherit money, others marry it. The majority work for it. We all spend it. We all want more of it.

"The love of money is the root of all evil."

In an age when the church is strangely silent on the subject, I would remind you that Jesus Christ had a lot to say about money, especially the peril of riches. The gentle and compassionate Saviour was hardhitting on the proposition: "You cannot serve God and money."

The deceitfulness of your pocketbook promises what it can never produce. Get wealth and then you will have prosperity, peace and influence. It just is not true!

"What can money do for you? Its roads are full of mirages, enticing gleams of water, which vanish as soon as we draw near. One after another the alluring pools turn out to be hot, glowing sand piles. The conditions into which riches lead you only intensify your thirst."

These men carry burdens which have all but crushed the spark of laughter. Millionaires often are staggering under the very thing which promised to carry them.

Men lay up for themselves by hoarding money. Men lay up for God by giving and sharing.

God gives to some the honor of having riches but He would give all His children the wealth of a contented life. This is wealth without limit.

"I know how to be abased and live humbly in straitened circumstances, and I know also how to enjoy plenty and live in abundance. I have learned in any and all circumstances, the secret of facing every situation, whether well-fed or going hungry, having a sufficiency and to spare or going without and being in want. I have strength for all things in Christ Who empowers me" (Phil 4:12-13, Amplified).

THE PERIL OF SUCCESS

"A bird in the hand is worth two in the bush: mere dreaming of nice things is foolish; it's chasing the wind."
ECCLESIASTES 6:9 (Living Bible)

A basic desire of man is to achieve.

Be sure to be on the top of the heap! So screams the world that bows and scrapes at the shrine of the goddess of success.

Keep on your toes. Put your best foot forward. Lead with a stiff upper lip, and keep abreast of the times. Use your head. Keep your eyes and ears open and your mouth shut! Elmer Wheeler calls this the anatomy of success.

Out of the pages of the Old Testament walks King Uzziah. As long as he sought the Lord, God made him to prosper. He was marvelously helped till he was strong. Then it happened. Success not only went to his head but spread like leprosy to his pride-filled heart.

"When he was strong, his heart was lifted up to his destruction: for he trangressed against the Lord his God" (2 Ch 26:16). He was carried away a leper, dishonorably discharged from the service of the Almighty. In gaining success he lost out with God.

His was no mere chasing the wind. Uzziah could never be accused of dreaming of nice things. He was a doer, a man of action. Success in itself was not his problem, but in achieving it he failed to watch and pray.

The dream becomes a reality of strength and success, producing a self-reliance and self-confidence that easily kills the dreamer. Confidence in one's own resources can easily wean a man away from an hourly trust in God.

But there is even a greater storm-brewing hazard in having a bird in the hand over two in the bush. You begin to use your power, privileges, and personality for self rather than for the blessing of others less fortunate. The moment you become ingrown you are ready to fall off the ladder of success. The higher you climb, the greater are the dangers.

The quest and achievement of life only finds its fulfillment in God. The ravenous appetite of a sick soul needs this comfort:

"This lawbook you shall never cease to have on your lips; you must pore over it day and night, that you may be mindful to carry out all that is written in it, for so shall you make your way prosperous, so shall you succeed. These are my orders; be firm and brave, never be daunted or dismayed, for the Eternal your God is with you wherever you go" (Jos 1:8-9, Moffatt).

TRIUMPH OUT OF TEARS

"Sorrow is better than laughter: for by the sadness of the countenance the heart is made better."
                              ECCLESIASTES 7:3 (Amplified)

All sunshine and blue skies make for a Sahara desert.

There must be the fall and winter to have a bountiful spring. Sweet wine comes from crushed grapes. Perfume, bread, paper, and steel are all the result of grinding, mashing and pressing.

For this very same principle in life, Solomon tells us in Ecclesiastes 7:3 that a funeral is better for man than a festival. Triumph comes out of tears!

Qualities of greatness in character do not come out of skit night, comedy hours and slapstick artists on a variety program. God's school for His men has daily courses on such applicable subjects as: how to handle pressure; what is the meaning of suffering; why do I have such difficult circumstances? learning the whys and wherefores of death.

Sorrow is better than laughter; indeed this is a paradox of the Christian philosophy of life. The Bible lays terrific emphasis upon joy, happiness, merriment and contentment in relaxed living. Why is gravity and seriousness better than a good, hearty laugh?

Sorrow produces a quality of character that is lasting. Verses two and three use a couple of expressions that bear this out: "The living will lay it to his heart" and "The heart is made better." Sorrow deepens the heart, grief stretches the heart, seriousness settles the heart and heartache flushes the heart.

"Now obviously no 'chastening' seems pleasant at the time: it is in fact most unpleasant. Yet when it is all over we can see that it has quietly produced the fruit of real goodness in the characters of those who have accepted it in the right spirit" (Heb 12:11, Phillips).

Sorrow is also not just an end in itself, it is a process. The cocoon is designed for struggle, not to kill, but in order that after the conflict there may come forth a beautiful butterfly. God takes us through difficulties so that He might bring us out on the other side to the praise of His glory!

Sorrow is better than laughter for it drives us to a sense of utter dependence upon God. Based upon 2 Corinthians 12:9-10 we come up with a concept that says: No sorrow, no dependence. No trials, no trust.

If we are strong, He is weak. When we are weak, He is strong!

A PROPER PERSPECTIVE

"Be not righteous over much . . . be not over much wicked."
ECCLESIASTES 7:16-17

Preserve the golden mean between excess and defeat!

Here in the seventh chapter, Solomon is admonishing us that both in well-doing and in evil-doing there may be overdoing that ends in undoing. There is danger in going too far and in stopping too short.

Is it possible to be too religious? This caution is against the counterfeit righteousness of talking too much, mere outward show, the emphasis upon the externals, legalism pressed out of measure and proportion.

"Over much righteousness" are the trifles magnified unduly. The rules and regulations of Christian living become the priorities. "This overdose of true Christianity is not the excess of godliness but the misdirection of it, the exhausting of it in the vanity of a man's selfish exploitation."

This is not a challenge against too much righteousness. "We cannot love God too warmly, nor honor Him too highly, nor serve Him too earnestly, nor trust Him too implicitly, nor pray to Him too assuredly. Our prime duty is to love Him with *all* our heart, soul, mind and strength."

This is a challenge against the formalist, the externalist, the insincere possessor who would use Christ and His church but refuses to be used by Christ and His church.

Then, there is the "over much" of wickedness. Is there a little sinning that is OK? Is balance in transgression permissible? Every sin and vice is "over much." This is warning against the flagrant sins, that which causes the murderer to die an early death.

The heavy drinker, "the wild and woolly son" who plows his hot rod into a bridge abutment at ninety miles per hour, the pride of Herod, the malice of Haman, the lust of Samson, the appetite of Esau or the sexual desires of Delilah are the "over much" of willful indulgences which easily slam shut the door of God's grace and forbearance.

"Learn to be truly righteous and truly holy. . . . Needed is a religion of reality, the stamp of God upon your heart and life" (Charles Bridges).

THE GRIM REAPER ARRIVES

"There is no man that hath power over the spirit to retain the spirit; neither hath he power in the day of death: and there is no discharge in that war." ECCLESIASTES 8:8

In London there is a business that has this strange sign over the entrance:

> We dye to live, we live to dye;
> The more we live the more we dye;
> The more we dye, the more we live.

Over the heart's door of Mr. Everyman hangs the sign: "A time to die." The struggle may be long or short, successful or failure, happy or sad, but the issue is certain. The word has gone out for all to hear, "It is appointed unto men once to die."

We live as if we are never going to die. We act as if we have an exemption from this universal law. We can forget death, ignore death, resist death, but "there is no discharge in that war."

Death is a battle that must be fought by every man. "There is no sending to that war," no substituting another to muster for us, no champion admitted to fight for us.

"The power of governmental leadership, that sways millions with a nod, fails here. The wealth of the materialistic board chairman, that procures for its owner all that his heart can wish, fails here. The might of the imperialistic warrior, which hath slain his thousands, and which no human arm could withstand, fails here. Physician, orator, and saint alike, even with the most earnest desire of life, and the tears, and the wailings, and the fond caresses of disconsolate affection—all fail here" (Wardlaw).

King Jehoram was thirty-two years old when he took the throne. Second Chronicles 21 tells the story of his utterly tragic life. He spent all his time squeezing the most out of the present and made so little preparation for after his death. At the age of forty he died with this epitaph: "He departed without being desired."

Forty years of living so intensely, so strenuously, cramming life full of things, but no time for God. Many a man, like Jehoram, has learned how to live but failed in knowing how to die.

In the military, discharge places a man beyond the point of death, but not here.

"Make me to know, O Lord, my end, and the length of my days, what it is. Let me know how transient I am" (Ps 39:4, Berkeley).

AN EASYGOING TOLERANCE

"Because sentence against an evil work is not executed speedily, therefore the heart of the sons of men is fully set in them to do evil." ECCLESIASTES 8:11

Keeping short accounts is a key to successful leadership.

Because we do not want to hurt a man's feelings, we allow things to build up. Because we are afraid to move in on a given situation, we delay necessary action. Because of a soft heart and often a spineless will, we permit someone to "get away with murder."

Whoever the offender is, this easygoing tolerance can be a curse to him and oneself.

Habits are not formed in a day. They are gradual and progressive. One of the greats of the church of England during the first part of this century was Bishop Taylor Smith. His analysis of man's plight was put this way: "Sin is at first very pleasing, then it grows easy; then it becomes delightful, then frequent, then confirmed. Then the man is unpenitent, then obstinate, then he resolves never to repent, then he is damned. Needed in the church of God are men to resist the beginnings."

Beware when we cease to warn men of that first step! Watch out when we keep silent when we ought to speak up against an evil work. Heaven help us when shame, remorse or the humble heart is missing in the disciplining of our sons and daughters.

Man goes on in false sincerity, because he goes on unpunished and unwarned! True, God is merciful, patient, and longsuffering, but how different would the Holy Scriptures read—

- if Lot's wife had gotten away with her backward look of self-centeredness and unbelief!
- if Achan's transgression of Joshua 7 had been condoned as a minor misdemeanor, and God had merely slapped his moral wrist!
- if Korah, Dathan and Abiram (Num 16:23-35) had the steam taken out of the sentence by the modern philosophy: "They are such fine fellows, and since it is their first offense, let's overlook this petty affair"!
- if Ananias and Sapphira were allowed to get away with their cheap dedication and poisonous proposition (Ac 5:1-10)!

Where are the faithful men to lovingly and firmly execute the sentence?

"If we confess our sins, he is faithful and just to forgive us our sins, and to cleanse us from all unrighteousness" (1 Jn 1:9).

A LIVELY OPTIMISM

"For to him that is joined to all the living there is hope: for a living dog is better than a dead lion." ECCLESIASTES 9:4

Enthusiasm is infectious! It is great to meet a man who is really alive. Put his success story under the microscope and you will often find that sustained enthusiasm is a big chunk of it. A spirited, vivacious and lively optimism is a keynote of the Christian faith.

It is impossible to be under the heat of Christianity and come out cold. An indifferent, unconcerned, reluctant "dead lion" is a contradiction in terms; that man would be a living monstrosity.

The "live dog" fervor is earmarked by three qualities: an overmastering acceptance of the greatness of God and His cause; a glow of emotion arising from that knowledge; and a consciousness of obligation.

Meet the Saviour. He will kindle your heart and set you free. When your earthly fire is lit from His divine altar all things are possible.

The "living dog" zeal that we approve is called "wholehearted consecration." Let it be emotional and tinged with loudness and boldness, and there will be those throwing verbal stones and sticks of "ridiculous exaggeration and fanaticism."

Beware of that which is shallow and undisciplined. Beware of that which is dead. Surface impressions and passing passions caused men and women one day to shout: "Hosanna, King of the Jews!" but the very next day these same "dead lions" were crying: "Crucify Him, crucify Him."

Life must have direction. Tragic to Solomon was consuming passion without constraining principle. Zeal is usually unconsecrated when related to a movement or "materialism" rather than to the Master. Doctrine, denominational establishment, financial security—enthusiasm inspired basically by these motives always will end in a desolating reaction.

"Life is Christ. Any enthusiasm for Christianity, apart from utter consecration to Him, can be a positive menace to the kingdom of God."

"I am come that they might have life, and that they might have it more abundantly" (Jn 10:10).

BE A FINISHER

"Whatsoever thy hand findeth to do, do it with thy might."
ECCLESIASTES 9:10

Thackeray's picture of unconcerned indolence is "a lazy slouching boy, with big feet trailing lazily one after the other, and large lazy hands, dawdling from out of tight sleeves."

Business, industry and the church are full of such boys, grown men with the temper and spirit that leads to our tragic Americanism, "Oh, that's good enough."

One of the most fantastic stories in the Holy Scriptures has to do with Nehemiah, the general contractor for the rebuilding of the Jerusalem wall. Here is the concluding remark: "So the wall was finished" (Neh 6:15).

The impossible was completed in fifty-two days by a man who cared and dared.

"Though you may have known clever men who were indolent, you never knew a great man who was so; and when I hear a young man spoken of as giving promise of great genius, the first question—I ask about him always is, 'Does he work!'" (Ruskin).

Luke, the physician; Paul, the tentmaker; Peter, the fisherman; Joshua, as chief of staff; or Gideon, the farmer, were all men who refused to do things by halves. Whatever their hands found to do, they did it with zest.

I have personally found that inefficient production, half-baked daydreams, poorly checked daily schedules and the "just get by" plateau, are answered by Tom Buckner when he tells me:

"Most affairs that require serious handling are distasteful. For this reason, I have always believed that the successful man has the hardest battle with himself rather than with other men. To bring one's self to a frame of mind and heart and to the proper energy to accomplish things that require plain hard work continuously is the one big battle that everyone has. When this battle is won for all time, then everything is easy."

Win the battle. Get victory over a half-a-mind, faint heart and lame endeavor. The pace and pattern of maturity can be summed up in the phrase: "Let not thine hand be slack."

"Whatever you do, put your whole heart and soul into it, as into work done for the Lord" (Col 3:23, Phillips).

SHELVED WITHOUT APPRECIATION

"There was a little city . . . Now there was found in it a poor wise man, and he by his wisdom delivered the city; yet no man remembered that same poor man." ECCLESIASTES 9:14-15

This is the tragedy of the forgotten man.

Many situations have been salvaged by the wisdom of some little fellow who is immediately overlooked and shelved although his contribution leads to triumph.

A few, feeble and frightened people once upon a time realized their tiny city was to be annihilated. No help was in sight. The battering rams of the mighty king of a foreign empire were being raised. Their village was to be wiped out without one chance for counterattack. The odds were staggering. Impossible were the chances for escape.

But for a poor wise man. Man sees the mighty king with his fabulous army and equipment. God sees the poor little citizen with a wise heart and mind.

One poor wise man with no profit figured out a weakness in the enemy's attack. There was a hole in the strategy. One insignificant native turned the tide of battle, and victory was assured the beseiged city.

The muscle man and his horde were conquered but "No man remembered that same poor man."

No reward, no honor, no civic dinner decorated their hero. Evidently he returned to his poverty and obscurity. He was shelved without a word of appreciation.

Joseph knew a little of this disappointment. He saved a mighty empire, he refused sin with the leader's wife, he redeemed the king's butler from prison, "yet did not the chief butler remember Joseph, but forgat him" (Gen 40:23).

Thousands of years have not changed the hearts of men. We still depend upon strength, weapons of warfare and the cry of him that ruleth among fools. (Study Ecclesiastes 9:16-18 as a contrast of wisdom to man's methods.)

"But God has chosen what the world calls foolish to shame the wise; he has chosen what the world calls weak to shame the strong. He has chosen things of little strength and small repute, yes and even things which have no real existence to explode the pretensions of the things that are—that no man may boast in the presence of God" (1 Co 1:27-29, Phillips).

A MIGHTY BIG STINK

"Dead flies cause the ointment of the apothecary to send forth a stinking savour: so doth a little folly him that is in reputation for wisdom and honour." ECCLESIASTES 10:1

Ointment plus dead insects equals a big stink!

If that equation bothers you, King Solomon comes up with a personal and practical application that really hits home. A Christian man of repute plus a little sin equals a spoiled and stinking report.

Insignificant habits, minor sins, unnoticed traits, hidden corners of life can spoil the whole thing like one drop of poison in a cup of water. It is not enough that we be sincere, but we must also be without offense.

The big sins of murder, social injustices or adultery are not the only ones that stink. Just as offensive are the lustful eye, the hasty word, the irritable temper, the rudeness of manner, the occasional slip and the supposed harmless eccentricities.

David took just a little look at his neighbor's wife.

Lot's wife took just a quick glance back toward Sodom.

Ananias and Sapphira withheld just a minimum amount of their gift.

Samson told a woman just a harmless secret he had with God.

Demas forsook the apostle Paul for a brief fling into the world.

Moses' flare of temper in striking the rock was such a speck of reaction.

All these biblical characters had a tremendous reputation till "the dead flies got into the ointment pot." Perfumes were commonly kept in sealed alabaster jars or cruses under the watchful eye of the perfumer or apothecary. It was only through carelessness that a fly could fall into the jar.

Leave the lid off your thought life and the lustful flies will start the mental rot. Neglect the sealing of your heart from impure motives and desires, and it will not be long before the aroma is sickening. Do not excuse, forget or become careless about the specks, fragments, mites and miniatures in your personal life. Plug the hole in the dike of your personal holiness and daily devotions to Almighty God. It has been the neglect of these little follies that has washed out many a good and great man for God.

"Take us the foxes, the little foxes, that spoil the vines: for our vines have tender grapes" (Song 2:15).

THE COST OF KINDNESS

"If the boss is angry with you, don't quit! A quiet and kind spirit will quiet his bad temper." ECCLESIASTES 10:4 (Living Bible)

An unkind Christian is a contradiction!

Kindness is the fabric of a big man. This sympathetic nature is not stuffiness or Pollyannaism, but a sincere attitude of love toward others.

If longsuffering is love in the passive, kindness is love in the active voice. Is the boss angry? Kindness is ready in attitude, voice and spirit. It is the feet and heart of Christian exercise.

"Be kind toward one another, tenderhearted, mutually forgiving, even as God has in Christ forgiven you" (Eph 4:32, Berkeley).

God takes notice of kindnesses done to others.

If you show compassion only to the boss who is worthy of it, what merit has that? Supposing God showed kindness only to those men who deserved it, where would we be? As tough as it is, we are to love our enemies. We are to do deeds of kindness to the stubborn, the rebellious, the hostile, even when he is our boss!

True humility is never artificial. Its genuineness is proven by the willing sacrifice, for the kindness that costs nothing is usually worth nothing.

In Bible times, if a poor man had no coals for a fire in cold weather, he would go out into the streets and beg. He would carry a pail on his head and let his need be known. As he passed by the house of one with whom he had been at odds, and that man was a Christian, there was only one thing to do. The Christian would take some live coals from his own fire and drop them out of his window into the beggar's pail. Thus he would "heap coals of fire on his head" and make himself a friend for life by this ungrudged kindness.

"The fruit of the Holy Spirit is love that issues in kindness."

Look today for an opportunity to relieve the sick, comfort someone in sorrow. Help shoulder the load for another man who is staggering, or by kindness and quietness in speech, quiet an upset friend.

Kindness is not the effeminate expression of weakness, but the demonstration of the gentleness of strength. Be big. Be kind!

"But the wisdom that comes from heaven is first of all pure and full of quiet gentleness. Then it is peace-loving and courteous. It allows discussion and is willing to yield to others; it is full of mercy and good deeds. It is wholehearted and straightforward and sincere" (Ja 3:17, Living Bible).

SHARPEN YOUR AXE

"If the iron be blunt, and he do not whet the edge, then must he put to more strength: but wisdom is profitable to direct."
ECCLESIASTES 10:10

Blunt and dull are the tools of the unskilled and lazy workman. He has never learned the lesson that preparation is more important than perspiration, that the emphasis must be upon skill rather than on strength, that brains can save muscles.

Daily there is the tragic possibility of doing the right thing in the wrong way, putting forth immense effort which ends in nothing since the iron remains blunt.

How sharp is the cutting edge of your life? How often we hack and chop away at life insensible to the fact that what we are is far more relevant than what we do.

Moses is a case in point. God ordained him to be the deliverer of the Jewish nation. At forty years of age, Moses set about to be this self-styled emancipator. But the iron was blunt. He tried his way, not God's. Forty years later, after many carborundum experiences down on Jethro's desert whetstone, Moses came back as a new sharp sickle honed for action.

A missionary in India came upon a helpless man sick of consumption. Nearby, sitting on a bridge, were two so-called "holy men" going through their prayers. The missionary called the two men to help him remove the ailing one to a shaded area. The only response was, "We are holy men. We never do anything for anybody."

William James, the famed Harvard University psychologist, insisted that the primary criterion of truth was that it should work. Reduced to common language, pragmatism is nothing less than the practical application of revealed truth.

God has given to every man three emery wheels for whetting the edge to a keen point. The Word of God, the disciplined practice of prayer and the person of the Holy Spirit. Wisdom senses when things are blunt and ill-defined in life. Take time out today for sharpening.

"Not by might, nor by power, but by my spirit, saith the Lord of hosts" (Zec 4:6).

WINSOME SPEECH

"The words of a wise man's mouth are gracious."
ECCLESIASTES 10:12

Have you stopped to taste your words recently? What flavor do they have?

Nothing is more detestable than tasteless speech.

The words of a wise man are not necessarily intellectual, clever, exciting or earthshaking. But they are always gracious, "kept wholesome and pleasant to the listening taste by the grace around it, and makes a man say something about truth that is attractive to the appetite of the hearer."

"Most men pay less attention to their words than any other area of life. They go through each day, speaking and talking without thought or reflection, and seem to fancy that if they do what is right, it matters but little what they say" (Moule).

A great deal of professed Christianity among men is not vital, because it is not vocal. There may be lots of small talk, cheap talk, loud talk, impressive talk, shady talk but little or no gracious talk.

Because there was no grace in his speech, Moses lost his heritage in the promised land (through anger). Samson lost his power and strength through loose talk. Saul lost his kingdom through deceitful language, Haman lost his life on the gallows through lying, Peter lost fellowship with the Master through proud and cocky chatter, Paul lost the brother relationship with Barnabas through self-centered differing.

In contrast, it was said of Jesus, "They all remarked about Him and wondered at the gracious words that flowed from His lips" (Lk 4:22, Berkeley).

Gracious words are sensibly tactful. This wise man knew how to avoid contention, his answers suited to the need, he resisted impatience and he would not spoil the harmony with intrusion of harsh and discordant notes.

His words were helpfully wholesome. This wise man used his speech for healing, not hurting; for building, not cutting; for sweetness, not poison.

Gracious words are lovingly winsome. Christ has speech that draws rather than repulses. "Speak pleasantly to [the non-Christian,] but never sentimentally, and learn how to give a proper answer to every questioner" (Col 4:6, Phillips).

"Set a watch, O Lord, before my mouth; keep the door of my lips" (Ps 141:3).

A CHEERFUL OPENHANDEDNESS

"Cast thy bread upon the waters: for thou shalt find it after many days." ECCLESIASTES 11:1

In the Near East, when the grain has been scattered over the fields, a flood of water is sent over the land, changing it for a time into a shallow lake. The seed seems to be lost. After a few days or weeks the water soaks in, green shoots appear under the hot sun, and harvest is assured.

King Solomon uses this illustration to demonstrate that God is no man's debtor. You cannot outgive God!

Give freely. It all may seem thrown away and lost. Some men will tell us, "Only a senseless fool could do such an unwarranted act of financial sowing."

Those men are a hundred per cent wrong! Nothing is thrown away that is done for God.

Teaching a class of high school boys? Laboring in a difficult church situation? Financing some folks in a remote and "impossible" mission station? It is not lost! The principal, plus interest, will return if lent to the Lord. Most of us are afraid of liberality. Hence, life is harvestless because of scanty sowing.

"Cast thy bread." Trust it to the waters. It will not rot nor disappear forever. One wise businessman, knowing how the winds of misfortune blow and knowing that his present prosperity might dwindle and disappear, built his successful life on this principle, "I possess nothing so completely, as that which I give away."

The Holy Bible teaches, that which you give, that you possess. That which you cling to, that you have lost! Examine such passages as Luke 6:38, and Proverbs 3:9-10; 11:24-25.

"Thou shalt find it after many days." God's timing is always best. It will return, perhaps not even in your lifetime or generation. The Chinese have a proverb that states it very well: "Long voyages make the best return."

Have patience. That which is apparently lost is deposited, and in God's own good time it will produce a most luxuriant harvest. Paul cast his bread upon the waters of many oceans, seas, continents and capital cities. Two thousand years later he continues to reap. "Let us not be weary in well doing: for in due season we shall reap if we faint not." (Gal 6:9).

"Happy and fortunate are you who cast your seed upon all waters, [when the river overflows its banks; for the seed will sink into the mud and when the waters subside will spring up; you will find it after many days in an abundant harvest]" (Is 32:20, Amplified).

INITIATIVE IS UNPOPULAR

"Young man, it's wonderful to be young! Enjoy every minute of it! Do all you want to; take in everything, but realize that you must account to God for everything you do."
ECCLESIASTES 11:9 (Living Bible)

The businessman who plays the game of conformity and produces for the organization is rewarded with automatic salary increases, easier hours, liberal vacations and an exciting pension plan. But the constriction of his independent spirit is the cost.

Conformity brings with it comfort, ease, laziness, and lack of purpose. The spark of achievement often is doused. Initiative is unpopular. The hardworking, God-fearing man is considered by many to be an oddball, and as common as a short-necked giraffe.

When war broke out between Spain and the United States, it was very necessary to communicate quickly with the leader of the insurgents. Garcia was somewhere in the mountain vastness of Cuba. No one knew where. No mail or telegraph message could reach him. The President must be sure of his cooperation and quickly.

What to do? Who would go?

Someone said to the President: "There is a fellow by the name of Rowan who will find Garcia for you."

Rowan was sent for and given a letter to be delivered in person to Garcia. Rowan took the letter, sealed it up in an oilskin pouch, strapped it over his heart, in four days landed by night off the coast of Cuba from an open boat, disappeared into the jungle, and in three weeks came out on the other side of the island, having traveled a hostile country on foot, and delivered his letter to Garcia.

President McKinley gave Rowan a letter to be delivered to Garcia. Rowan took the letter without asking: Where is he? How do I get there? Is there any hurry? Who will help me? Why can't Charlie go instead of me?

Carry a message to Garcia! We do not need more education, more instruction, more experiences or more incentives, but a stiffening of the vertebrae which will cause us to be loyal to a trust, to act promptly, to concentrate all our energies.

Take the initiative. Be willing to concentrate on a task and do it. You are accountable only unto the Lord.

"Whatever you do, put your whole heart and soul into it, as into work done for the Lord, and not merely for men" (Col 3:23, Phillips).

WE BECOME WHAT WE ARE

"Remember now thy Creator in the days of thy youth."
                                        ECCLESIASTES 12:1

How frightful is the delusion: Let the devil have the prime and God the dregs. Youth is for pleasure, middle age for business, and old age for religion—so they say! How can we expect God to help in old age if we will have nothing to do with Him when we are in our prime?

He gives Himself most to those who give themselves early.

Begin in the beginning of thy days to remember Him from whom thou hadst thy beginning and go on according to that beginning, keep Him in mind, never let go.

Take a look at the figurative picture in verses 2-7 of a patient in some convalescent home:

"The sun, moon and stars be darkened." Sight is dim, their countenance is clouded and the lustre is gone from their personality.

"The clouds return after the rain." The old man has just got over one pain or ailment and another one attacks.

"The keepers of the house tremble." The head, arms and hands are shaky and feeble. Strength from the guard is gone, the vigor is sapped!

"The grinders cease because they are few." The teeth are few and far between or else they are gone altogether. Digestion becomes a major problem.

"Those that look out the windows are darkened." The light of the eyes is dimmed and glasses become almost a necessity.

"The doors are shut in the streets." The easy-flowing speech of early years is gone. The battery is running down and words give place to meditation.

"They rise up at the voice of the bird." Sleep becomes difficult and early wakefulness becomes a pattern. Little things disturb.

"They are afraid of that which is high." They lose their enterprise. Frightened by heights, their heads become dizzy.

"The almond tree flourishes." The head becomes covered with snow-white hair.

"The grasshopper is a burden and desire fails." Little things sink an old man and the ambitions of youth are tasteless.

Hearken to the words of Gipsy Smith: "Save an old person and you save a unit, but save a young man and you save a whole multiplication table."

GOADS AND NAILS

"The words of the wise are as goads, and as nails fastened by the masters of assemblies, which are given from one shepherd." ECCLESIASTES 12:11

The old tradesman was resting during his lunch hour with a sandwich in one hand and a much-worn Bible in the other. His cynical boss came by and remarked, "How can an old codger like you understand the Bible?"

With the grace of a Christian gentleman, the old man replied, "It would not be possible, sir, in the ordinary way; but you see I happen to know the Author!"

This is the devotion to the God that makes this book at home in the palace of the Queen of England or on the coffee table of the coal miner's cottage in central Pennsylvania. Its appeal is to all.

The Bible was written by inspired kings, statesmen, soldiers, philosophers, priests, scholars, poets, physicians, tentmakers, herdsmen and saints. Sections of the Bible were written in the desert of Sinai, in the wilderness of Judea, by the river of Babylon, in a dungeon at Rome and on the lonely island of Patmos.

Sixteen hundred years span the beginning with Moses and the conclusion with John. Contents include history, biography, legislation, poetry, philosophy, doctrine, ethics and perfect guidance for personal, civic and national life.

One theme, one subject, one objective—how do you explain it? "Holy men of God spake as they were moved by the Holy Ghost" (2 Pe 1:21).

Solomon calls these men "masters of assemblies." They were leaders of men, not mere secretaries or human electronic machines transmitting a divine message. They were ordinary men with the touch of the extraordinary God upon their hearts, minds and hands.

God's Word serves as a goad. It can be useful to urge the sluggish forward or to give correction and rebuke which pricks the heart, not the skin.

It also serves as a nail to anchor us to God.

GOD'S ORIGINALITY FOR YOU

"Let us hear the conclusion of the whole matter: Fear God, and keep his commandments: for this is the whole duty of man. For God shall bring every work into judgment, with every secret thing, whether it be good, or whether it be evil."
ECCLESIASTES 12:13-14

It is a sad day when man must ask: "To whom do you belong?"

It will be a sadder day when God brings every work into judgment, yes, even every secret thing.

It is tragic when men lose their identity through compromise. There is very little left in a man's daily life that makes him distinguishable.

In politics compromise leads to deceit and faithlessness to the voters. It is the ignoring of campaign promises, the igniting of the fuse that destroys character and deadens conscience.

What is the conclusion of the whole matter as far as Solomon was concerned? Do not give in or give up for that which is less in value. Do not set aside convictions and basic committals of life for that which is hazardous and objectionable.

"Fear God and keep His commandments." That simply means to love the Lord and do whatever He says. This is the whole duty of man. Do that and you have it made for sure.

But by and large we think we know better and it is not long before we are so involved and mixed up that our component parts are no longer seen or heard. Biblically it is termed: "unequally yoked" (2 Co 6:14).

Yoked—so tied into intimate association that freedom is lost, purposes are restricted, and God's originality for you is surrendered. An ox and an ass plowing together is a monstrosity. Wheat and tares have no alliance. Dirt in the cement makes the bonding impossible.

Be a man in the world, but beware of being one of them. Mingle but do not unite in marriage, business deals, social commitments, civic responsibilities—"Don't let the world around you squeeze you into its own mold, but let God remold your minds from within" (Ro 12:2, Phillips).

Strip your whole life down to the two basic principles: Fear God and keep His commandments. Love Him and obey Him! To whom do you belong? Admit it and show it.

"With these promises ringing in our ears, dear friends, let us keep clear of anything that smirches body or soul. Let us prove our reverence for God by consecrating ourselves to Him completely" (2 Co 7:1, Phillips).

Part 5

A CHALLENGE FROM ISAIAH

when the ceiling is zero

It has been suggested that there are close to seven thousand promises in the Bible. From Genesis to Revelation the Bible is the story of God's gifts being graciously bestowed. The promised land for the children of Israel was the land of fantastic promises. "Every place that the sole of your foot shall tread upon, that have I given unto you, as I said unto Moses" (Jos 1:3).

The book of Isaiah can be a workshop for learning to claim some of the great promises of Almighty God. As you read, claim the promises and give God the chance to prove Himself faithful to His Word. Mark in your Bible the date that you claimed the promise, then memorize the verses you have taken.

As you pray, take the promise that God has given you and believe that He will fulfill it. Then keep a file of answered prayers, promises proved. It will encourage you in times of discouragement.

REMOVE THE SCARLET HUE

"Come now, and let us reason together, saith the Lord: though your sins be as scarlet, they shall be as white as snow; though they be red like crimson, they shall be as wool." ISAIAH 1:18

A crossless and sacrificeless Christianity is a lie. Hebrew writers of the Old Testament invariably thought of religious ideas in terms of pictures. Thus, when they thought of sin, they did not think of a mere theological abstraction but of a heavy burden which needed to be lifted, a crooked way from which men needed deliverance, and a foul stain from which they need to be cleansed.

This is the amazing invitation of a holy, righteous and sinless God saying to mankind, "Come." The Almighty is giving every sinner the same invitation, which is also to be considered a command to enter into judicial proceedings. He is not inviting men to a discussion but to a court trial. This is the righteous judge of the universe inviting us to stand before Him with Jesus Christ, His Son, as our Advocate and Substitute.

This is the gospel of redemption. God recognizes our fallen condition. He also knows we are helpless sinners who can never change scarlet into white nor crimson into wool.

But "Christ receiveth sinful men." He came to remove the crimson stain. He came to make the foulest clean.

Dr. A. T. Pierson throws much light on this lively invitation for cleansing. He tells us that the passage carries us back to the craft of the ancient dyers. So impressed were they with scarlet and crimson that they supposed it was impossible to extract such colors from any fabric which was affected by them, and he reminds us that it is just over one hundred years ago that the method of bleaching scarlet rags was discovered.

If it were impossible to remove the scarlet hue and the crimson stain from a fabric, what must have been the difficulty in removing sin from the soul of man! Isaiah the prophet is magnifying the grace of God and the sublime miracle of redemption. This fabulous promise reminds us daily of Jesus Christ who alone is able to save to the uttermost, and whose precious blood can make the foulest clean.

Whenever you take a good, healthy look at the religions of the world, or modern philosophies of life, one of your first questions should be regarding its treatment of sin. What message of cleansing and redemption does it contain? Does it diagnose the malady, and does it satisfactorily prescribe a remedy?

It is God alone who can make the scarlet as snow and the crimson white.

A MOBILE STRIKING FORCE

"Also I heard the voice of the Lord, saying, Whom shall I send, and who will go for us? Then said I, Here am I; send me." ISAIAH 6:8

Do you consider yourself a part of this available pool of manpower so drastically needed by God in our generation? Or let me put it to you another way, do you have the spirit of the volunteer, a minuteman for the Almighty? Are you willing not just to go for the glorious, well-paying jobs but to pay the price, regardless?

Passive obedience says, "Here am I."

Active obedience says, "Here am I, send me."

Often the curse of the expendable attitude is the entanglements of life—finances, family, poor health, desire for security, lack of training and education, or perhaps, an unwilling heart for service.

Do not get involved in things which will hold you back. How often men have told God, "Lord, I would sure like to do that, *but*—Many a *but* has kept a man unavailable.

God may never ask you to go, but constantly He is asking you *to* be willing. The willingness to go any place, at any time, with anybody (or even nobody) and under any circumstances is absolute submission in faith to God's directions.

Nineteen hundred years ago, down alongside the seashore, Jesus said to two brothers, "Follow me." Immediately their hearts and souls responded. They secured their jobs with relatives and we read these words in Matthew 4:20, "And they straightway left their nets and followed him."

This is scriptural maneuverability. These disciples, Peter and Andrew, became the inner core of Christ's mobile striking force to a pagan, religious, commercial and military world.

Some men are available but not prepared to go. Others are prepared but not available. Not so the Gadites! These were fighting men who responded to the need of King David (1 Ch 12). Available in the hour of need, their secret is hidden in three little phrases of that chapter:

"they were not of double heart" (vs. 33).

"they could keep rank, and came with a perfect heart" (vs. 38).

"were of one heart" (vs. 38).

God needs your availability. How does your heart respond?

"And he trembling and astonished said, Lord, what wilt Thou have me to do? And the Lord said . . . , Arise, and go into the city, and it shall be told thee what thou must do" (Ac 9:6).

AN IMPOSSIBLE BIRTH

"Therefore the Lord himself shall give you a sign; Behold, a virgin shall conceive, and bear a son, and shall call his name Immanuel." Isaiah 7:14

The incarnation is full of the impossible! It is almost too fantastic to be real. The Bible states as facts many incidents that can only be classed as unbelievable by human judgment.

Hundreds of years before Christ's birth is the story of His supernatural birth, life and redemption on Calvary's cross.

God Himself gave the sign and named the child Immanuel.

All this happened right on schedule, "in the fullness of time." Jesus was to be born in one of the tiniest countries of the Mediterranean world in an obscure little village to an inconspicuous peasant woman.

There is the miracle of His virgin birth. The seed of the Christ child was of the Holy Spirit, or in the medical statement of Luke: "For with God nothing shall be impossible" (Lk 1:37).

This is not the language of theory but the language of fact! Jesus was not the son of Joseph but the Son of God. Christ was not God-and-man nor man-and-God. He was God-man.

There is the miracle of His mission. Jesus was born that He might die! My pattern, teacher, leader, and friend became my Saviour through His redemptive death.

His amazing virgin birth and the wonder of Immanuel, "God with us," transcends all the wonders of the world. It is unexplainable and inexplicable.

But here is the miracle that surpasses all miracles. It is found in 2 Corinthians 5:21:

Christ knew no sin—the miracle of a sinless Saviour.

Christ made Himself sin for me—the miracle of His substitutionary sacrifice.

I have been made the righteousness of God—the miracle of a saved and redeemed sinner!

GULP A TRANQUILIZER

"Thou wilt keep him in perfect peace, whose mind is stayed on thee: because he trusteth in thee." ISAIAH 26:3

This promise sounds so idealistic as to be impossible, especially in these days of unrest and instability. Pressure of circumstances, burdens of anxiety, pessimism about the future, dark and depressing inner thoughts can warp and unnerve you in materialism's outlook.

To find relief, millions of tense and worried men have begun taking tranquilizers. Across the heart-door of this tired, nervous, fearful and fretting creature is hung the card, Do Not Disturb!

These drugs called ataraxics (a term derived from the Greek word meaning, "not disturbed") have a way of screening out feelings of worry, fear, and anxiety. The result is a sense of peace, relaxation, and well-being.

But true peace can never be purchased at the corner drugstore.

There is also a false peace called prosperity. It is based on the shaky hopes of the fool's paradise, materialism. Many fellows would rather trust in their old enemy than put full confidence in their only true Friend. Are you grasping a broken reed or gripping the solid Rock?

Peace is not selfish sloth or inactivity. The tranquility of an enchanted isle of somewhere is a peace found by escaping reality to a country hideaway.

But, Christian peace is not found in a pill, nor in prosperity, nor in some place, but rather in the Person and Presence of God Himself. He guards your inner citadel!

Peace is a quiet, calm and unhurried resting upon your heavenly Father. He is the author of peace (1 Co 14:33). This verse in Isaiah actually says in the Hebrew language: "Thou keepest in peace, peace; a peace that is perfect, without one ripple of anxiety, the mind of the one leaning hard upon Thee."

Note the emphatic individuality. Though everyone else is trusting the Lord, and you are not, their companionship and atmosphere will profit you nothing. Your heart must rest and wait in Him.

Perfect peace is the Christian's unique possession. It is unbroken by changing conditions of life.

AWAIT FURTHER ORDERS

"He that believeth shall not make haste." ISAIAH 28:16

Have you read recently in the Bible about Egypt's Pharoah chasing after his departed bricklayers? Read all about it in the book of Exodus, chapter 14.

About two million refugees had been told by God to leave the land of fish, cucumbers, melons, leeks, onions, and garlic (Num 11:5). The evacuation is recorded in history as the exodus. As they headed east, following the cloud by day and pillar of fire by night, they suddenly came upon the shores of the Red Sea.

With water in front and Pharoah's forces behind, they were caught in the middle!

The Almighty God told them to stand still. As a mouse in the trap, or a lonely lamb cornered by a lion, there they were. It was time for God to do a miracle. There was no other hope.

Pharoah, fear, frustration are no real peril if God has spoken. The children had come to the end of the line, but for God! A man is prone to measure God either by his knowledge or his ability to scheme out of tight spots. We see alternatives: desert, sea or enemy. God sees the fourth: a miracle.

When God tells you to stand still, He then encircles and protects.

When God tells you to be, He then will give you the power to become.

When God tells you to go, He opens a path through the sea.

Right now you may not know what to do. It looks dark and threatening. Let God take the initiative. If you will wait, God will work! Cease from your trying. Start to trust and praise Him for what He is going to do.

Your enemy whispers to you: "Waiting means that you are doing nothing. Give up, throw up the white flag of surrender." Impatience suggests: "Stir yourself. Go jump into the sea."

If you look at the Red Sea, the approaching enemy or yourself, you will want to die right there in the desert, but for God! You will be able to wait if you trust the Promiser and know He keeps His promises.

Do not interpret God's command to wait as passivity, negligence or nonchalance. *Stand still* is not a mood of do nothing. Surely our miracle God does not want it to be a time of dull discouragement of things as they are, rather an eager anticipation of what is about to happen.

Stand still and wait for further orders.

"For God alone my soul waits in silence" (Ps 62:1, Amplified).

COCOON STRUGGLE

"And therefore will the Lord wait, that he may be gracious unto you, and therefore will he be exalted, that he may have mercy upon you: for the Lord is a God of judgment: blessed are all they that wait for him." ISAIAH 30:18

In God's laboratory of building men, strengthening character, healing spirits and restoring confidence, He has a very important area called the waiting room!

Impatient, nervous, fidgety, we often enter unwillingly, hating to admit that a great deal of life's time is made up of waiting—waiting for a plane or train, waiting to see the doctor, waiting to receive a letter, waiting to recover from sickness, waiting to find a new job, or just waiting for something to happen!

We wrestle with this entire process of waiting. It is so much easier to be doing, to be active.

Impetuous youth says, "Go, man, go!" Maturity and wisdom says, "Wait. Take time. Hold tight!" God says: "Blessed are all they that wait."

It is tough enough to wait for that plane or letter, but how we chomp at the bit waiting for God to make His next move.

Can you imagine Abraham waiting till he was over a hundred years old for the birth of his first son? Or Moses waiting forty years in the desert? How difficult it must have been for the children of Israel to stand still on the shores of the Red Sea with the Egyptians moving in behind them!

The discipline of waiting does much for God's man. It teaches him patience and faith (Ps 27:4); it enables him to watch God at work (Ps 62:5); it matures him through struggles and stress as the butterfly coming from the cocoon (Is 64:4). And best of all, the man who waits has the touch of God upon his life (Lam 3:22-27).

Think on this—God waits so He may be gracious to you. Happy, satisfied and completely honored in this confidence is the man who will wait for Him. He waits for you. Will you wait for Him?

"But they that wait upon the Lord shall renew their strength" (Is 40:31).

AT THE FORKED ROAD

"And thine ears shall hear a word behind thee, saying, This is the way, walk ye in it, when ye turn to the right hand, and when ye turn to the left." ISAIAH 30:21

When in doubt as to the correct course of action, here is a precious promise of God's guidance and direction. "The Lord shall guide thee continually." Businessmen would find their burdensome transactions smoothed and successful if they would take time each day to seek guidance from God.

Lock your door. Open your Bible before you, open your heart in prayer, thus seeking divine guidance for each day.

Men make mistakes. I question if you would make nearly as many if you would take the time to seek His counsel and obey the Word which says, "In all thy ways acknowledge him, and he shall direct thy paths" (Pr 3:6).

Most of us can settle issues that are clearly right or wrong, but the dilemmas of life are in the conflicts between right and right. At the forked road both directions seem to be OK.

Then the fog settles down and both roads are closed. What does one do now? How is the will of God determined under such difficult circumstances?

It is never so dark, so difficult, so desperate that you cannot hear the voice of God speaking. Those who are to be guided must be in a personal relationship with the guide. Know Him, love Him, and be prepared to carry out His every instruction.

James McConkey puts it on the line: "Guidance is one of the severest tests of the Christian's walk with God. It touches his life at every point. Prayer; knowledge of the Word; personal temperament; tendency to haste; advice of friends; reliance upon our own wisdom; impatience with delays; submission to the will of God in all matters in question . . . all these become factors in seeking guidance and they test to the limit our personal walk with God."

Here are a few time-tested guideposts to look at when you are wondering whether it should be the right hand or the left that you take—the counsel of a wise friend, the check of a God-controlled conscience, confidence in the leadership of the Holy Spirit, hints of Providence, advantages of day-by-day opportunities, and the supreme and final authority of the Bible.

"I will instruct you and train you in the way you shall go; I will counsel you with My eye on you" (Ps 32:8, Berkeley).

THE CREAM OF GOD'S LOVE

"O Lord, be gracious unto us; we have waited for Thee."
                                             ISAIAH 33:2

The story of human history tells of man's need of God's free grace.

There is no story so thrilling and exciting as the story of grace! Life, health, friends, prosperity, church and the presence and influence of our Bible are all tokens of the common grace of God for mankind.

"O Lord, be gracious." In grace, God's thoughts become gracious actions. It is not only how He feels, but also what He has done. His longsuffering and forbearance are smothered in grace. Grace is not just a gift of things, but the gift of a Person.

Whether it be an attribute of the Godhead or free and unmerited favor in spontaneous action, it points to one thing—all that a Christian man has or is centers exclusively in Christ and depends entirely on God through Christ.

In 1785 Robert Hall wrote: "The whole system of the Gospel is emphatically the Gospel of the grace of God. It is an exhibition of unmerited favor to a guilty and perishing man; all the blessings which it proposes to bestow, all the helps it inspires, are ascribed to this as its origin. The grace of God is the only thing which can correct the evils that prevail among mankind."

Here are some challenging definitions and descriptions of grace:

Grace is God's heart of love poured out to me as a sinner, in spite of my heart of hatred to Him.

Grace is the cream of God's love, life with the spiritual vitamins from the heart of God, able to destroy every germ of sin.

Grace simply points me to the Lord Jesus Christ on the cross of Calvary.

The law of Moses demanded righteousness. All we sinners can do is plead: "O Lord, be gracious unto us." God under grace makes His righteousness the free gift. The law blesses the good. Grace saves the bad.

You need not, indeed cannot, attempt to do anything for your salvation. God has done it all. This is the grace of our Lord Jesus Christ.

"For the grace of God . . . teaches us to have no more to do with Godlessness or the desires of this world but to live, here and now, responsible, honourable and God-fearing lives" (Titus 2:11-12, Phillips).

QUIETNESS THAT QUICKENS

"And the work of righteousness shall be peace; and the effect of righteousness quietness and assurance for ever."
                                                              Isaiah 32:17

How little stillness there is in our lives. It is difficult to learn the lesson that there is a time to hurry and a time to slow down, a time for noise and a time for silence, a time to speak and a time to listen.

The man who has a period of silence at the beginning of each day is wonderfully impressive. Righteous men are always found to be peaceful men, quiet men and assured men. This takes time alone with God in personal devotions. The quiet place is always the place of revelation. Give Him that unruffled opportunity to speak, to lay out His plans for the day and then time to empower you for action.

Such silence and quietness is your greatest need but also your greatest time battle. We do not want to stand still, to be calm, to be ready to hear the voice of God. "Time out" with God can be a thrilling or a quivering experience. "But the Lord is in his holy temple: let all the earth keep silence before Him" (Hab 2:20).

Our concept of time has us attempting to get each new day off to a fast start. Come out of your bed like a sprinter and never dare let down until you collapse into bed at night.

Wise men set a pace. The first hour should be for warming up the motor, setting the sights, preparing the human machinery. Momentum is gained through the quiet pause that refreshes.

If it be true that we are in an age of permanent emergencies, then build into your daily life these precious minutes each morning that prepare you for battle. Can you afford to spend a few minutes each day for God? You cannot afford not to.

"But the one listening to me will dwell secure, will be quiet without dread of calamity" (Pr 1:33, Berkeley).

THE DISCIPLINE OF DEPTH

"Take root downward, and bear fruit upward." Isaiah 37:31

How absolutely foolish to build a house without first laying a foundation; to plan on a Ph.D. without going to school; or to desire a wheat harvest without first planting the grain.

The root system of life is a must! Everything in life depends and builds upon it. The mighty Sequoias of the Sierra Nevada Mountains can only go up in direct proportion to their growth downward. He who would reach great heights must dig deep!

Lack of roots is the cause of many a man's failure. This is dramatically seen in the aspen tree in the Rocky Mountain region. Groves of beautiful, white-trunked trees dot the mountains, but in heavy snows or sixty-mile-an-hour winds, they tumble down.

Why? Their root system is circular and shallow. They grow tall and top-heavy but have little to hold them in the hour of storm. No deep taproot anchors them in the blasting of adversity.

What man sees above the ground is really not the most important part of the tree. The spreading branches, the shapely leaves, and the abundant fruit are a result of something hidden underneath.

The man who concentrates on the root system of his life is going to bear fruit upward, but if he concentrates on the eye-appealing foilage he may end up a rootless failure.

The trees of Job's forest were felled. The axe of the enemy cut deep and sure. Seemingly, nothing remained for this giant of God but to decay and die. Not so! Job had built his root system deeply and solidly for years. Listen to these thrilling words in Job 14:7-9 (Berkeley): "For there is hope for a tree, if it is felled, that it will sprout again and that its shoots will flourish. Though its roots age in the earth and its stump dies in the ground, at the scent of water it will bud and branch out like a young plant."

"He is like a tree planted by water, that sends out its roots by the stream, and it does not fear when heat comes, for its leaves remain green; in the year of drought it is not anxious, for it does not fail to yield fruit" (Jer 17:8, Berkeley).

THE ONLY BOOK FOR EVERY MAN

"The grass withereth, the flower fadeth: but the word of our God shall stand for ever." ISAIAH 40:8

The Bible is often called "the Book for every man." Within its pages, every man can see himself, find the answers to his basic heart needs, receive encouragement, strength, heart-tranquilizing peace and best of all, he can be assured of a plan for the life hereafter.

This is the Book that continues to be the world's best seller and civilization's most important document. Yet amazingly, it is one of life's most neglected books.

Romanoff is not only a connoisseur of good eating but also a sharp observer. He said, "There are three publications we seldom plunge into. The dictionary, therefore we don't know how to spell. The cookbook, therefore, we don't know how to cook. The Holy Bible, therefore, we don't know how to find God."

The only volume that gives significance to our times gathers dust in the desk, library and hotel room. The only source for knowing God in a personal way continues to be neglected, while men look in vain to the sciences, philosophies and arts.

Why has the Bible stood forever? Because of what is in it.

One little girl was sure she knew what was in the family Bible. Carefully she described its contents to her pastor, "Sister's baby picture, a lock of hair and a recipe for mother's upside-down cake. Oh yes, a pressed violet." What is in your Bible?

It is God's picture book for man to see Him and himself. It is the encyclopedia of heaven for eternal information. It is the divine dispensary for medication and therapeutic healing. Are you needing purposeful direction for this day? Here is a guidebook for individual answers just tailor-made for you.

But there are strings attached. You must take time to open the Book, extract the truth and then apply. It is not enough just to know and maintain a theological vocabulary. You must act.

Man must do something with what God has given. The resources of God are yours for the taking.

"Open my eyes, that I may contemplate the wonders of Thy law" (Ps 119:18, Berkeley).

KEEP ON KEEPING ON

"He giveth power to the faint; and to them that have no might he increaseth strength. Even the youths shall faint and be weary, and the young men shall utterly fall: but they that wait upon the Lord shall renew their strength; they shall mount up with wings as eagles; they shall run, and not be weary; and they shall walk, and not faint." ISAIAH 40:29-31

Are you discouraged today? Has that "what's the use" attitude come over you? This promise from Almighty God tells us to stay with it; it is always too soon to quit.

The size of success is wrapped up in the active exercise of persistence. "Let us not grow tired of doing good, for, unless we throw in our hand, the ultimate harvest is assured" (Gal 6:9, Phillips). The question is not one of harvest, but of what will be the measure of our harvest.

We have a basic job to do—sow the seed. Be persistent. In the book of Ecclesiastes we are told about three attitudes that keep men from producing: (1) observing the wind, (2) regarding the clouds, and (3) knowing not the workings of God. They were easily discouraged because they lacked trust in God, who has promised the harvest.

Two factors must be kept in mind as we go about our task. First, sowing seed is hard work involving long hours. Work gratefully, not grudgingly. Work as a man, not as a machine. Be on top of your work, not under it.

Second, it is impossible to know if what you are doing is the best way to success. The key to triumph is in that first syllable, *tr(y)*. The sovereignty of God reserves the means and times of His worker's prosperity to Himself.

"Work: for I am with you, saith the LORD of hosts" (Hag 2:4).

A SHOT OF PENICILLIN

"Every one helped his neighbor and said to his brother, Take Courage!" ISAIAH 41:6 (Berkeley)

How much more effective is a pat on the back than a kick in the pants! It is an encouragement.

Work on this ministry of encouragement. Say a good word; commend a job well done; let men know they are appreciated. This encouragement is a balm to discouraged spirits and a tonic to the downhearted.

Note Isaiah 41:7, "The craftsman encourages the goldsmith, and he who polishes with the hammer encourages him who strikes on the anvil, saying of the soldering. 'That is good!' " (Berkeley).

See the big picture of what others are doing and be humble enough to say, "That is good."

Someone has said that people are like corn—they will live if planted and left alone. But that is not true. They need the encouragement of cultivation, sunshine and TLC (Tender Loving Care)!

Self-centeredness sees no good in others; Christlikeness says to his brother, "Take courage," and refreshes his heart by words of encouragement.

Encouragement must be more than mere words. Translate language into action. That pat on the back, the smile to the depressed one, the financial lift to the needy, befriending the outcast or being hospitable to the homeless.

The act of encouragement is an infusion of fresh courage and strengthening. When a man's heart is down, his feet are dragging and his spirits are low, what a shot to have a man speak words of encouragement.

Encouragement is like penicillin to younger men coming up. When a man is losing his grip on life, he needs a load-lifter, not destructive criticism or sarcasm.

Let your life be a constant encouragement to others. This means that you need your heart lifted before you can lift others. Learn from King David. He was in a serious predicament. Men were talking about killing him. All the people were in an ugly mood on account of the killing of their sons and daughters by the Philistines. Then this majestic statement in 1 Samuel 30:6, "But David encouraged himself in the LORD his God."

RETOOLING FROM THE INSIDE OUT

"Fear not, you worm Jacob. . . . I will change you to a sharp, new, threshing sledge, having cutting edges."
ISAIAH 41:14-15 (Berkeley)

Nobodies become somebodies through no work of their own—this is the thrilling news of Christianity to failures. God is in the business of transformation.

Have you ever read about a destitute bum becoming a fabulous millionaire? Do you know of a has-been salesman who is "the toast of the corporation?"

That is what this promise is all about, plus a whole lot more! God promised to change Jacob from a worm to a threshing machine, from that which is despised to that which is praised, from being walked upon to that which cuts a terrific swath in life.

Notice who is to accomplish this. Not hours of self-determination, religious Carnegie courses, or a secret formula on "How I Raised Myself by My Own Bootstraps"!

Lasting success is a result of God taking over in your frustrated life. "A holy process of new development, the bright antithesis to process of decay is now arrested and reversed. And best of all, this process is continuous" (Moule).

Jacob became Israel. This was a retooling from the inside out. When God takes over in your life, He renovates, remodels and completely refurnishes His men. Worms never become warriors except by the renewing grace of our living God.

The secret of success stories? God did it! Not by educational brilliance, abnormal talent, generous philanthropy, popular approval, fabulous wealth, moral excellence, religious fervor, amiable disposition nor untiring activity; none of these commendable qualities can make a man of God out of a worm! They are merely superficial, futile and inadequate.

Notice also into what the Almighty has promised to change you—not just an improvement on the old nor a reworking of the "worm." His workmanship is new, refreshing, invigorating, and recreating. The added fantastic guarantee is that you will be sharp and have that cutting edge to life.

"As Christ was raised from the dead by the Father's glorious power, so we too should live an entirely new life" (Ro 6:4, Williams).

DO NOT DARE TOUCH IT!

"I am the Lord, that is My name; and My glory I will not give to another nor My praise to graven images."
                                    ISAIAH 42:8 (Berkeley)

When men begin to praise, exalt, and glorify you—watch out! God does not share His honor nor does He divide up the praise. It is His, not yours! Keep your hands and heart off that which rightfully belongs to Him.

An outstanding Christian leader was being given an honorary degree from a school of higher learning. It was in recognition of his contribution to our generation, his influence upon the masses of humanity and his selfless efforts to bring men back to God. After much praise, honor and an overwhelming amount of scholarly dignity, Billy Graham made this statement:

"I humbly accept this honor on behalf of the One to whom it rightfully belongs. I am merely the vessel and instrument that God has seen fit to use. I will hold this degree temporarily until He returns and then together we will give Him the honor, the praise and the splendor that only He deserves."

Nebuchadnezzar tried to keep glory for himself, much to his deathly regret. Like a strutting peacock, this egotist said to himself, "Is not this great Babylon, that I have built by my mighty power as a royal residence and for the glory of my majesty?" (Dan 4:30, Berkeley).

But God refused to give Nebuchadnezzar the glory. The humiliation of animallike insanity was to teach him that his power was not his own, but delegated to him by God, the supreme ruler of the world.

King Herod tried to steal some of God's glory in Acts 12:21-23 (Berkeley): "The mob shouted, 'A voice of a god and not of a man!' But instantly an angel of the Lord struck him, because he did not ascribe the glory to God. He was eaten by worms and died." God refuses to release His glory to man.

The idea of the glory of God occurs over two hundred times in the Old Testament and some one hundred and fifty times in the New Testament. It is constantly before us on the pages of Holy Scripture as a reminder that the chief end of man is "to glorify God and to enjoy Him forever."

"So, whether you eat or drink or whatever you do, do it all to the glory of God" (1 Co 10:31, Berkeley).

THE ROUTE TO TAKE

"When thou passest through the waters, I will be with thee; and through the rivers, they shall not overflow thee; when thou walkest through the fire, thou shalt not be burned; neither shall the flame kindle upon thee." ISAIAH 43:2

Are you passing through some dark and terrifying tunnel? This verse tells about circumstances that have stopped mighty armies, but God promises you a way through. The trials and difficulties are not to be evaded but encountered. Do not run away from problems. By God's grace, run through them.

"For by thee I have run through a troop; and by my God have I leaped over a wall" (Ps 18:29).

Waters, rivers, fires, and flames are enough to stop any man. But God says, "through obstacles are not the end, but a means; not the conclusion but often a condition. They are the process, not the end product, the way, not the arrival, a pause, but certainly not the final period.

Pass through the waters with Him; you will not be swamped, but purified. Pass through the fires unharmed and emerge refined.

God Almighty, who knows the beginning from the end, promises to bring you through. Whether you are faced with the Red Sea, or trying to forge "the swelling of Jordan" or enduring a fiery furnace like the three Jewish lads, it is always great to cling to this promise: "I will be with thee; . . . they shall not overflow thee; . . . thou shalt not be burned."

Do you feel like you are in the frying pan? Never forget Daniel in that lion's den; David being chased by King Saul; Elijah alone for God on Mt. Carmel; Jehoshaphat pinned in by the allied armies; Gideon's army reduced to a meager three hundred men; or Jonah down inside that tremendous fish.

The Captain of our salvation, Jesus Christ, did not encircle or go around His adversities or headaches. Hebrews 2:9-10 tells us: "He by the grace of God should taste death for every man. . . . He was made perfect through sufferings." He tasted. He passed through!

"He knoweth the way that I take: when he hath tried me, I shall come forth as gold." (Job 23:10).

CLAIM AND CLING

"Remember ye not the former things, neither consider the things of old. Behold, I will do a new thing; now it shall spring forth; shall ye not know it?" ISAIAH 43:18-19

Man is always the loser if he fails to take advantage of the promises of God. In an hour when the skeptic is staggering, why do we see the man of God standing? The skeptic grasps at straws. The man of God clings to the promises.

In the midnight of circumstances most men fear the worst, but the Christian man finds his faith feeding on the promises of God. "Never doubt in the dark what God has promised in the light."

A promise of God is His guarantee, His pledge to act, His gift graciously bestowed. Fifty-two times in the New Testament the word *promise* is used. Never is it linked with a thought of negotiation on the part of man. God makes no bargains, and we can make none with Him.

The promises of God are free and unmerited if you will do three simple things: (1) comply with the conditions laid down; (2) pray the promise into your life; and (3) then, by faith, believe God!

Remind yourself that God has promised to meet your every need. Nothing is overlooked. Everything has been anticipated.

The Bible takes on new meaning when one comes to the place of realizing that God's promises speak to each person as an individual. He knows your name, your family, your circumstances, your problems, your weaknesses and your future. He has the answers for your every need. If you will only believe.

Do not look over your shoulder to the past. Look ahead.

Do not reflect, anticipate.

Ask God to challenge your heart with some of the thrilling promises in the book of Isaiah that have an eye for the future. Isaiah wrote during trouble-packed days. Religion, government, morality and ethical conditions were at an all-time low.

How delightful to hear God speak through this mighty prophet with promises for His children three thousand years later.

A POT OR PASSAGEWAY?

"Shall the clay say to him that fashioneth it, What makest thou? or thy work, He hath no hands?" ISAIAH 45:9

Here is an interesting test of success or failure: Are you a passageway or a pot, a thoroughfare or a dead end? Are you a channel through which your life flows to that of another?

The message from God through Isaiah tells us that a vessel of clay may be the instrument of God. You should not be complaining if you are clay and not gold.

When the opposition asked John the Baptist who he was, he simply replied that he was a voice. He did not claim to be a leader, organizer or advanceman, just a voice, the ventilator through whom the Lord would breathe His message.

We pray, "Lord, use me."

We need to pray, "Lord, make me useable."

Useable instruments are channels unclogged and clean.

Jacob had to be broken clay before he became a "prince with God."

Peter had to be humbled in his utter failure and selfishness before being used in effective action as a versatile vessel.

God had to bring Saul of Tarsus to the ground in helplessness and the cry of desperation, "Lord, what wilt Thou have me to do?"

Anything hallowed and available to serve as a receptacle, God will use. He took Moses and his rod, Gideon and 300 men loaded with lamps and pitchers, David and his slingshot, Peter's rude fisherman's boat, and the little Jewish boy's lunch of three loaves and two small fish.

God wants to use you! Are you willing to be a clay pot through whom the Almighty pleases to move and bless? As a tool in the hand of the wise Masterbuilder be serviceable.

God has fashioned you. God has created, formed and molded you for His glory. Be the best possible piece of clay available in the Potter's hands.

"This priceless treasure we hold . . . in a common earthenware jar—to show that the splendid power of it belongs to God and not to us" (2 Co 4:7, Phillips).

THE FURNACE OF AFFLICTION

"Behold, I have refined thee, but not with silver; I have chosen thee in the furnace of affliction." ISAIAH 48:10

When God refines a man there is no doubt that he has been refined! The flames of trial remove the impurities.

Just when it seems that all is lost, God's words come, saying, "I have refined thee.... I have chosen thee." The fire is not to kill or ruin but to build and bring forth a new and better life. Man sees all loss and doom. God sees refinement and purity.

Several years ago a group of businessmen bought a guest ranch in Colorado. On a June night, one of the guests was smoking in bed. A fire started, and the main lodge with housing facilities, dining room and kitchen, plus the recreational and lounge area, burned to the ground. Nothing was left but charred cement walls and dark, naked trees nearby. The hush of death was in the air.

But for God! Except for our confidence in our sovereign Lord there would be the temptation to throw up our hands in despair.

But for God! The refined silver was still there. He had graciously spared enough of the ranch that it could be rebuilt and continued. The storm had passed and they could truthfully say: "In every thing give thanks; for this is the will of God in Christ Jesus concerning you" (1 Thess 5:18). "Wherefore glorify yet the Lord in the fires" (Is 24:15).

Where there is life there is hope. There is a brighter future with God.

On the day of the fire, the reading in *Streams in the Desert,* a daily devotional book by Mrs. C. E. Cowman, had encouraged the director of the ranch. It said,

"Have you ever seen men and women whom some disaster drove to a great act of prayer, and by and by the disaster was forgotten, but the sweetness of religion remained and warmed their souls? God may not give us an easy journey to the Promised Land, but He will give us a safe one. In a thousand trials, it is not five hundred of them that work for the believer's good, but nine hundred and ninety-nine of them, and one beside."

May God enable us to see beyond the circumstances, furnaces of affliction, heartaches and tragedy to see that God is on the throne and that His way is perfect.

Surely, He will send the testing fires. The cheap tinsel and showy draperies of life go up in flames mighty fast. God is concerned about gold and silver.

"Every thing that may abide the fire, ye shall make it go through the fire, and it shall be clean" (Num 31:23).

POLISHED UP OR POLISHED OFF?

"And he hath made my mouth like a sharp sword; in the shadow of his hand hath he hid me, and made me a polished shaft; in his quiver hath he hid me." ISAIAH 49:2

Never steal tomorrow out of God's hand!

What God is doing today has the payoff in the tomorrows of your life. Today there may be the crucible of fire and testing so that tomorrow God will have a weapon of dependability.

In the shadow of His hand, in the darkness of His quiver—these are places of preparation for usefulness. God always takes time in qualifying an instrument for service.

The thought of being a sharp sword or a polished shaft sounds marvelous, but we rebel against the little phrase: "He hid me." That suggests obscurity, and obscurity means darkness, the unknown, the uncertain. No applause, no popular approval, no acclaim!

Obscurity means time apart from people and the crowd. We are more anxious for public display than time alone hidden in the shadow of His hand. "Do not run impetuously before the Lord; learn to wait for His timing; the minute hand as well as the hour hand must point to the exact moment for action."

Never forget that you are in "His hand" and in "His quiver." Only there can Almighty God make a man into a sword and shaft. Do not resist what He is attempting to do with you.

Polishing the shaft hurts, but it produces a godly luster. Some lives are "polished off" while others are "polished up." The result of polishing up is reflection, and a glorious sheen.

"The fining pot is for silver, and the furnace for gold: but the Lord trieth the hearts" (Pr 17:3).

Swords and arrows are not to remain in the sheath or the quiver. Both are built for action. Allow God to make you today into whatever He can use for the tomorrow of His will.

FASTENED TO THE FIXED

"For the Lord God will help me; therefore shall I not be confounded; therefore have I set my face like a flint, and I know that I shall not be ashamed." ISAIAH 50:7

Rare is the man that is fastened to the fixed! There are days for men to latch onto temporal sky hooks. They will take hold of anything if it might swing a better deal. Like a fluttering butterfly, most fellows are flicking through life, seeking that which will satisfy the appetite.

Promises of "pie in the sky" are not stable enough to anchor your hopes to. Circumstances are far too relative. Success has no fixed point. Money? Solomon could rightly testify: "Wilt thou set thine eyes upon that which is not? for riches certainly make themselves wings; they fly away as an eagle toward heaven" (Pr 23:5).

Is your heart fluctuating and your soul slipping? Why not try anchoring your life on the eternal and unchanging God? Wise men throughout the ages have built upon this Rock. He alone can give you stability and an unashamed outlook on yourself and life.

The secret? Jesus Christ, the Son of our living God, is the foundation laid for all men's security. Footings of life are solid when founded upon Him. Ideas, theories, and opinions are easily swept away by changing winds, but the great affirmations of the Christian faith shall stand!

"If we have nothing abiding beyond this perishable material universe, it would indeed be misery to exist. Life would be not only insignificant but wretched, and a ghastly irony, a meaningless, aimless ripple on the surface of that silent, shoreless sea. . . . Let the mountains crumble and the hills melt away; beyond the smoke and conflagration, stands the throne of Almighty God, life's great unshakeable. God is in control and His name is Everlasting."

What is your measure of anchorage? Are you set like a flint, unashamed? "I say only this, let the builder be careful how he builds! The foundation is laid already, and no one can lay another, for it is Jesus Christ himself" (1 Co 3:10-11, Phillips).

Be that man who is fastened to the fixed, that man who has established his life upon the unmovable. The Lord will help you not to be confounded nor ashamed.

"He shall not be afraid of evil tidings: his heart is fixed, trusting in the LORD. His heart is established, he shall not be afraid" (Ps 112:7-8).

OVERSTUFFED COMPLACENCY

"Listen to me, you who follow after righteousness, you who seek the Lord; look to the rock from which you were hewn and to the quarry from which you have been dug."

ISAIAH 51:1 (Berkeley)

One of the deadliest of all diseases in America is complacency. In this day of overstuffed living and self-satisfying attitudes, it is good to remember from where God has brought us.

Dr. Henry Smith Leiper, a leader in the American Bible Society, has given us a wonderful picture of the world by reducing proportionately all the people of the earth into a theoretical town of a thousand. He tells us it would look something like this:

In this town, there would be 60 Americans; the remainder of the world would be represented by 940 persons. The 60 Americans would possess half the income of the town, with the 940 dividing the other half.

About 330 people in the town would be classified as Christians. Fewer than 100 would be Protestant Christians, and some 230 would be Roman Catholics. At least 80 townspeople would be practicing Communists, and 370 others would be under Communist domination. White people would total 303, with 697 nonwhite.

Half of the thousand would never have heard of Jesus Christ or what He taught. On the other hand, more than half would be hearing about Karl Marx, Lenin and Stalin.

The 60 Americans would have an average life expectancy of 70 years; the other 940 averaging less than 40 years. The Americans would have an average of 15 times as many possessions per person as all the rest. The Americans would produce 16 percent of the town's total food supply. Although they eat 72 percent above the maximum food requirements, they would either eat most of what they grew, or store it for their own future use at enormous cost.

Since many of the 940 non-Americans in the town would be hungry most of the time, it could lead to some ill feeling toward the 60 Americans, who would appear to be enormously rich and fed to the point of sheer disbelief by the great majority of the townspeople.

The American families would be spending at least $850 a year for military defense but less than $4 a year to share their religious faiths with the other people in the community.

"Hold back no benefit from those entitled to it, when it is in the power of your hand to perform" (Pr 3:27, Berkeley).

LOOK FOR THE KING'S WINE

"I, I am He who comforts you; who are you that you should fear mortal man?" ISAIAH 51:12 (Berkeley)

Comfortable living does not consist in the possession of comfortable things.

Electric heat, warm shower baths, breakfast in bed, air conditioning in the new car—these are a few of the external "extras" that help make living a little more enjoyable but not necessarily do they give internal comfort.

Ralph Barton, one of the nation's top cartoonists, left this note pinned to his pillow before committing suicide:

"I have had few difficulties, many friends, great successes; I have gone from wife to wife, and from home to home, visited great countries of the world, but I'm fed up with inventing devices to fill up twenty-four hours of each day."

He was influential and popular—yet lonely, burdened, discouraged, and comfortless. Despite all his possessions, Barton did not know the comfort of Christ.

The original meaning of *comfort* suggests the impregnable protection of a mountain fortress.

We are swept off our feet by the death of a loved one; we are plunged into despair by poor health; financial reverses shatter our hopes. When all seems lost we need to sense a new and invigorating resource. "I, I am He who comforts you."

When God comforts, He gives strength in weakness. God protects where we are exposed. God comes alongside and pours in the oil of gladness and reinforces the foundational footings. He does not remove the cross: He gives strength to bear it. He does not stop the battle: He gives peace in the midst of war. He does not take away the adversity: He gives courage to endure.

Samuel Rutherford encourages man's heart with this comforting advice: "Whenever you find yourself in the cellar of affliction, begin to look around for the King's wine."

Here is some that was bottled two thousand years ago and gets better as it ages: "Blessed by the God and Father of our Lord Jesus Christ, the merciful Father and the all-comforting God, who comforts me in every sorrow I have, so that I can comfort people who are in sorrow with the comfort with which I am comforted by God" (2 Co 1:3-4, Williams).

GOD NEVER PANICS

"For you shall not go out with haste, nor shall you go by flight . . . for the Lord will go before you, and the God of Israel will be your rear guard." ISAIAH 52:12 (Amplified)

Here is a statement which challenges the quick, bustling, feverish spirit of our times. The man, who is accelerated in his busy life by a blast of hurry and estimates progress by speed and noise, knows little of this promise.

Seemingly, the race is to the swift and the battle to the strong. Lead in the pants or wings on the feet may both be wrong. Dragging one's feet or hot-footing it through life may keep a man from being in step with God.

Urgency is one thing, but the hurry and bustle caused by fear and terror is quite another. Slow down. The man who would be guarded by God must find His pace and then keep in step.

A life that is always too busy for quiet deliberation and unhurried calm loses out in three areas:

1. There is no time for prayer and meditation. Your talks with God are mostly a P.S. as you hurry out the door or into another meeting.

2. You leave God behind, for He is in no hurry, nor does He panic into sharp decisions.

3. Like a whirlwind, you leave things behind in a mess.

One hundred years ago in central China, a pioneering missionary named Hudson Taylor was impatient. He thought he needed more assistants, more money, more medical supplies, more of everything from England. Months rolled by and nothing came— no help, no money, no supplies!

There, alone with God and the Bible, amidst millions of Chinese, Taylor discovered a basic principle for his future life and mission: "He that believeth shall not make haste" (Is 28:16).

Progress seems so slow. Learning that fruit takes time to ripen is difficult. First the blade, then the ear and then the full ear of corn. This runs contrary to our twentieth century "blast of hurry" living.

The promise tells me that God is in front and behind. He sets the pace, and He seals the rear guard. He is the Alpha and the Omega. He guides up front and forms the protection on the rear flanks. He sees ahead and watches behind. And where am I? Right in the middle!

LEARN FROM THE LAMB

"As a lamb that is led to the slaughter and as a sheep before her shearers is dumb, so He opened not His mouth."
Isaiah 53:7 (Berkeley)

Silent submission is not a quality of the milk-toast nor is meekness a sign of weakness.

Little men push themselves to the forefront. Big men allow their lives and deeds to do the preaching. Weakness has to defend itself; strength has already spoken.

The prophet Isaiah is telling us about the Lion of the tribe of Judah (Jesus Christ) who one day in the future would take the place of a lamb. The howl and growl of the king of beasts would give way to silence and submissiveness.

The King was to be killed, and He pleaded not His case.

The Leader was to be crucified, and He offered no self-defense.

The Son of God was to be murdered, and all of heaven kept quiet!

How else could He have reacted?

He could have reminded the soldiers of who He was and the power at His command. He could have told the Jewish leaders to reread their Scriptures—in particular that fifty-third chapter of Isaiah. He might have pleaded with the frenzied mob not to allow the Innocent to die, the perfect One to be purged, their best Friend to be betrayed. He might have organized His band of disciples into an army of counterrevolutionists and, with a sneak attack, foiled the plot of the religious leaders.

Blown His stack! Told them off! Put them in their place! Used every vocabulary power at his command to talk Roman and Jewish high command into a stay of execution!

But the perfect Lamb of God knew when not to talk, not to act, not to command.

Learn from the Lamb. There is a time to speak, and there is a time to shut up.

"In the multitude of words there wanteth not sin: but he that refraineth his lips is wise" (Pr 10:19).

SEE IT BIG!

"Enlarge the space of your tent, and stretch out the curtains of your dwelling; do not hesitate, but lengthen your cords and make secure your tent pegs!" ISAIAH 54:2 (Berkeley)

"Young man, sit down! When God pleases to convert the heathen, He will do it without your aid or mine!" Young, enthusiastic William Carey was squelched by the presiding preacher at the minister's meeting. His passionate plea, his staggering vision was ignored.

He sat down, disappointed but not discouraged, for he was sure of his ground. On that August 10, 1786, Carey was silenced for a moment, but only for a moment.

He saw a world unreached except by materialistic trading companies. He was stirred in his heart to take action for God and he had been assured by promises of God from sacred Scripture. Six years later, Carey brought an epoch-making message from the above text and epitomized it in two memorable exhortations:

Expect Great Things From God.
Attempt Great Things For God.

This quiet, plodding shoemaker from Hackleton, England dared to believe God. He considered the "practicability of something being done for the conversion of the heathen."

Note in this promise of God, the vision is for expansion, not retreat, recession nor seclusion. "Break forth on the right hand and on the left" is the standing order of the day.

Note the urgency involved—"do not hesitate." How the hot heat of godly enthusiasm is iced over by the cold logic of practical difficulties! Have you caught yourself saying: "It can't be done. That's impossible. Who am I to be trying that? And anyway, there's no money to start with. Let's wait and see."

"There are moments when the faith of one man is contagious, and the strength of one becomes the strength of many." Move forward on the highway of faith and others will follow.

Note the necessary balance in these words from Isaiah—lengthen the cords and secure pegs! "Strengthen the stakes" refers to a solidly anchored personal life. When this is driven deep and fast, then the ministry follows. You can only go up and out in direct ratio to your going down with the pegs of life.

Have you extended yourself too far? Are you pretending to be something you are not? Strengthen the stakes of your life today! Vision is only visionary without the foundation of biblical intake and prayer-filled uplift.

HOLIDAY OR HOLY DAY?

"If thou turn away thy foot from the sabbath, from doing thy pleasure on my holy day; and call the sabbath a delight, the holy of the Lord, honourable; and shalt honour him, not doing thine own ways, nor finding thine own pleasure, nor speaking thine own words: then shalt thou delight thyself in the Lord."
ISAIAH 58:13-14

How do you observe Sunday, the Lord's day? The first day of the week was made for you. It was meant to be a boon and not a burden, not a holiday but a holy day. It is not twenty-four hours taken away from man by God but a day given by God to man for his delight.

This day is a provision from the Almighty who knows our needs for rest, relaxation and renewal. "While your heart is opened to the Lord in worship, your mouth opened in witness, your pocketbook opened in giving ... heaven will also be opened in blessing."

The manager of a popular golf course is reported as having said, "Even if these business executives don't need one day off in seven, our putting greens do!"

Sunday is for rest and relaxation, getting refreshed. It is an opportunity for those burned out by busyness to take time out to get together with God.

Sunday is for readjustment and reevaluation. Rested and reassured from the Word of God, perspective is possible for the new week's pursuits. Sunday is God's prescription for "this strange disease of modern life with its sick hurry and its divided aims."

Thomas Edison warns us that the laws governing the universe would call for a halt in the progress of science in the interests of parallel moral advance.

Halt one day each week. Let your soul catch up with the rest of you.

Need there be a code of prohibited practices, thus making Sunday a "No-You-Can't-Do-That Day"? Let this be a day when you practice worship according to the dictates of the Holy Bible and your heart. Work develops the physical; but worship develops the character. This is the crying need of men today.

The infidel, Voltaire, revealed satanic strategy, when he wrote: "You can only destroy Christianity when you first destroy the Christian's Sabbath." By means of accelerated sports programs, unnecessary labor, studying meant for the six days and self-gratification, we have made common that which God says is holy.

If Sunday is His, allow Him to have it. Seven days a week for sure, but this one in particular.

HOLD THE ROPES

"And he saw that there was no man, and wondered that there was no intercessor." ISAIAH 59:16

In the year 1792 the shoe cobbler, William Carey, was discussing the gospel opportunities with his friend Fuller. "The gold mine of India seems as deep as the center of the earth . . . who will venture to explore it?" Carey was quick to answer his own question. "I will go, but you who remain at home must hold the ropes."

Holding the ropes is persistent and persuasive intercessory prayer—praying for others, sharing the burdens, appearing at the throne of grace on behalf of another, advocating as does the honest lawyer.

"Where there is no intercessor, men perish." We get so wrapped up with our needs, problems, and desires that we completely neglect interceding for others.

"But intercession is an inescapable obligation. Christ "ever liveth to make intercession for them" (Heb 7:25).

Be specific. Intercede for particular needs of your friends, your family, your working partners. Beware of generalities. Intercessory prayer changes things and it changes people. "Powerful is the heartfelt supplication of a righteous man" (Ja 5:16, Weymouth). Stimulate your prayer life by looking out, looking around, and looking abroad, rather than just looking introspectively within.

There is a terrific value in a written prayer list. It rescues you from selfishness. "Hold the ropes" for missionaries, pastors, Christians from other lands, and military personnel around the world. Does your interceding for others have an Acts 1:8 flavor? Beginning at home base, do you pray for the "uttermost parts of the world"?

"The Lord turned the captivity of Job, when he prayed for his friends" (Job 42:10). In answer to your prayers, what has ever happened or been accomplished for God? Power flows through the yielded man when he is interceding for others. Focus on points of concentration in prayer. Kneel to conquer for Christ!

Remember, you cannot ask too much from our all-powerful King.

"God forbid that I should sin against the Lord in ceasing to pray for you" (1 Sam 12:23).

GEOMETRICAL REPRODUCTION

"A little one shall become a thousand, and a small one a strong nation: I the Lord will hasten it in his time." Isaiah 60:22

Mathematics is the key to success in God's economy. He subtracts when there is a liability (Ac 5:1-11). He adds daily to the record book those who are assets (Ac 2:47). He divides when provincial thinking and cloistered living exist (Ac 8:1).

But God's master strategy of penetration and world conquest is as old as creation: "Be fruitful, and multiply." (Gen 1:28). Multiplication was God's first command to man. It has remained on the divine statute books forever as scriptural mathematics.

Man's way of increase is an arithmetical principle: one plus one equals two. God's ways of increase is by the geometric ratio. "A little one shall become a thousand." The results are viewed not on the basis of mathematical activity but geometrical reproductivity. He looks at not just number but quality, not just volume but net profit, not just addition of names but multiplication of the lives transformed.

One shall become a thousand. We should be vitally interested in that kind of percentage profit for the kingdom of God.

The farmer can take three hundred and sixty kernels of wheat, plant them, and in the fall harvest about eighteen thousand kernels. This is God's eternal way.

He took Gideon, discarded the arithmetical principle and with three hundred won a stunning upset. Was Gideon a fool? Yes, except for this promise of geometrical victory: "A small one shall become a strong nation."

Men who believe God *are* something and will surely *do* something! They are men who desire to be multiplied!

Do you feel little? God can make you a thousand. Do you feel small? God will make you a strong nation.

"I tell you truly that unless a grain of wheat falls into the earth and dies, it remains a single grain of wheat; but if it dies, it brings a good harvest" (Jn 12:24, Phillips).

THE FARCE OR FORCE OF PRAYER

"It shall come to pass, that before they call I will answer, and while they are yet speaking, I will hear."
ISAIAH 65:24 (Berkeley)

God has promised to beat us to the draw!

Before the call is uttered, the answer is on its way. The suddenness of the answer to our prayer makes us conscious that we should have asked sooner.

A band of prayer warriors gathered in the home of Mary. High on the priority list was a preacher named Peter in prison. His release was urgently requested. While they were beseeching, God was acting. Peter was miraculously released. You can read about this jailbreak in Acts 12:1-19. Peter immediately went to the home of the prayer meeting and knocked on the door.

There stood the answered prayer, but no one could believe it. They had prayed for the impossible and their answer came too soon.

"Peter continued knocking" (Ac 12:16). When the door was finally opened, the intercessors were astonished.

It is a *farce* to pray much, expecting little. Unbelief drags.

It is *force* to pray little and get much. Faith delivers.

Never forget that before you ask, your Heavenly Father knows that you have the need. It is for our good and His glory whether He answers now or later.

God's children stood frightened, strangely alone and forsaken on the west coast of the Red Sea. Before they called, God was answering with a strong east wind. The Lord's route through the midst of the waters on dry ground was not a bypass, nor a detour nor an afterthought.

It was His prepared-ahead-of-time highway that those million Jews had not even dared to dream about it. It was prepared but sent in answer to faith.

"Behold, I am the Lord, the God of all flesh: is there anything too hard for me? Call unto me, and I will answer thee, and shew thee great and mighty things which thou knowest not" (Jer 32:27; 33:3).

QUALIFICATIONS FOR LEADERSHIP

"I will look favorably upon that man who is humble, feels crushed in spirit, and trembles at My word."
                                    ISAIAH 66:2 (Berkeley)

The modern organizational man would find a great deal of difficulty in qualifying for this divine approval.

Industry smiles upon the go-getter, the self-starter, the human dynamo, the fellow with wide-range versatility, imagination and creativeness. This man is a sure bet! But he would flunk the Lord's critical appraisal techniques as mentioned in this our text from Isaiah. They might be good, capable, proficient men, but the Lord is scoring results on a far different basis. Notice the three basic qualities for which He is looking:

Humility, repentance, and sensitivity. For maximum effectiveness, these are the demands of God for top-flight men in His service.

Tragic is the cocky, proud and arrogant "I." This overdose of self-assurance leads to a terrific statement by A. W. Tozer: "Let the public accept a man as unusual, and he is soon tempted to accept himself as being above reproof. Soon a hard shell of impenitence covers his heart. He closes the coffin lid with these words: 'I am the foremost leader, I am not to be trifled with, my opinions are not to be questioned. If I do it, it is right!'"

God is looking for men with a sense of brokenness, a deep consciousness that he is far from what he ought to be. Humble self-distrust says, I have erred and am asking for forgiveness. I am ignorant and am willing to be taught. I am wrong and am willing to be corrected.

God looks favorably on any man who is sensitive to His holy Word. Willingness to have his heart massaged by the Scriptures does not make a humble man weak but rather shows him to be a man of conviction, purpose and one of heaven's "sure bets."

"For God sets Himself against the proud—the insolent, the overbearing, the disdainful, the presumptuous, the boastful, and opposes, frustrates and defeats them—but gives grace (favor, blessing) to the humble" (1 Pe 5:5, Amplified).